Also by Carol Cox
in Large Print:

Sagebrush Brides:
　Journey Toward Home

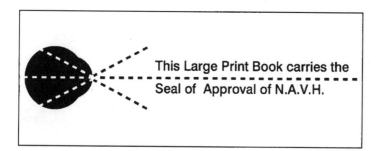

This Large Print Book carries the
Seal of Approval of N.A.V.H.

SAGEBRUSH BRIDES

The Measure of a Man

SAGEBRUSH
BRIDES
The Measure of a Man

Love Rules the Ranch

CAROL COX

**Large
Print**

Cox

Thorndike Press • Waterville, Maine

IWPL0010244726

Copyright © 1999 by Carol Cox
Sagebrush Brides Collection #2

All Scripture quotations are taken from the King James
Version of the Bible.

All rights reserved.

Published in 2006 by arrangement with
Barbour Publishing, Inc.

Thorndike Press® Large Print Christian Romance.

The tree indicium is a trademark of Thorndike Press.

The text of this Large Print edition is unabridged.
Other aspects of the book may vary from the original edition.

Set in 16 pt. Plantin by Minnie B. Raven.

Printed in the United States on permanent paper.

Library of Congress Cataloging-in-Publication Data

Cox, Carol.
    The measure of a man : love rules the ranch /
by Carol Cox.
        p. cm. — (Sagebrush brides) (Thorndike Press
large print Christian romance)
    ISBN 0-7862-8351-3 (lg. print : hc : alk. paper)
    1. Large type books. I. Title. II. Thorndike Press
large print Christian romance series.
PS3553.O9148M43 2006
    813′.54—dc22   2005031431

SAGEBRUSH BRIDES

The Measure of a Man

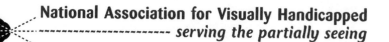
National Association for Visually Handicapped
serving the partially seeing

As the Founder/CEO of NAVH, the only national health agency solely devoted to those who, although not totally blind, have an eye disease which could lead to serious visual impairment, I am pleased to recognize Thorndike Press★ as one of the leading publishers in the large print field.

Founded in 1954 in San Francisco to prepare large print textbooks for partially seeing children, NAVH became the pioneer and standard setting agency in the preparation of large type.

Today, those publishers who meet our standards carry the prestigious "Seal of Approval" indicating high quality large print. We are delighted that Thorndike Press is one of the publishers whose titles meet these standards. We are also pleased to recognize the significant contribution Thorndike Press is making in this important and growing field.

Lorraine H. Marchi, L.H.D.
Founder/CEO
NAVH

★ Thorndike Press encompasses the following imprints: Thorndike, Wheeler, Walker and Large Print Press.

Chapter 1

Scattered clouds moved slowly across the sky, casting broad shadows on the grassland below. Occasional gusts of wind tugged at the red-checked cloths covering the tables set up end-to-end in front of the sprawling ranch house, but the weather didn't seem to dampen the spirits of the crowd gathered around the tables.

Hearty laughter burst forth from one end of the line of tables, where a group of weather-beaten cowboys sat. The high-pitched voices of children punctuated the buzz of conversation. Everyone seemed perfectly in tune with the lighthearted spirit of the day.

Everyone but the young girl seated near the head of the first table.

Lizzie Bradley toyed with her food, pushing bits of mashed potatoes, baked beans, and shredded beef around her plate with her fork. It didn't make an appetizing combination, but if the food was disturbed enough, she reasoned, maybe no one would notice that she had barely touched her dinner on this special day.

Overhead, the clouds gathered and thickened, marching in formation across the sapphire sky. The same procession had occurred daily for over a week now, but so far the summer rains had not materialized. Lizzie glanced up, trying to decide if these clouds meant business. She sighed inwardly. *It's hard to know about so many things.*

All around her she could hear the happy chatter of her family — her parents, her brother, her young cousins and their parents — and, in deeper tones, the good-natured banter of the ranch hands, who were always an important part of the annual barbecue at the Double B. Usually this cookout was a high point of Lizzie's existence; it reinforced a sense of security in their way of life on the ranch her father and uncle had built. This year, though, try as she might, she couldn't force herself to get into a festive mood.

What's the matter with me? she wondered. But she had no answer.

Her father rose to his feet, and the buzz of conversation gradually stilled. Charles Bradley's gaze swept over the gathering, and Lizzie felt a familiar twinge of pride at his ability to speak to a large group while making each person present feel that Charles was speaking directly to him or her.

"Folks," he began in a strong, clear voice, "we've come a long way since we first set foot on this land eleven years ago. We came here with three thousand cattle and our hearts full of dreams. God has been faithful beyond our hopes. The Double B is now running more than twenty thousand head of cattle on some of the finest range in New Mexico Territory. And we have working for us, without question, the best ranch hands in the country."

Hearty whoops of approval from the cowboys greeted that statement, and Charles, grinning now, waited for the roar to subside before he continued. "Abby and I have been blessed to watch our two children grow strong and healthy in this land."

Lizzie shot a quick glance at Willie, wondering if her younger brother felt as embarrassed as she suddenly did. Probably not, she concluded wryly. It took a lot to disturb Willie's sunny equanimity.

Her father was still speaking. "We've also been blessed to have my brother, Jeff, and his wife, Judith, as our partners and to watch their family expand." Lizzie covered a quick smile with her hand when she saw her aunt Judith blush at this reference to her obviously pregnant figure. True to form, her father went on smoothly, only a twinkle in his eyes betraying his amusement at Judith's discomfort.

"All in all, God has blessed us richly over the years, and we thank Him for His goodness. This fellowship meal is a very small way to express our gratitude for all of you who have worked so hard this past year."

Jeff rose to stand beside his brother. "I'm not the speaker Charles is," he said, "but then, few people are." He grinned as laughter quietly rippled among the tables. "But I want to add my appreciation to his for what you've done, all of you. The success of the Double B wouldn't have been possible without your help and loyalty, and we thank you." The brothers raised tall glasses of cider in salute just as a rumble of thunder clapped overhead loudly enough to rattle the silverware. Huge drops of rain spattered on the table.

Excited squeals from the children added to the commotion as chairs were quickly scooted back and everyone scrambled to lend a hand grabbing dishes, bowls, and utensils and hurrying them into the house.

The shock of the cool drops snapped Lizzie to attention, and she hastened to stack the dishes closest to her into two large serving bowls and gathered the whole load in her arms. Willie, enjoying the unexpected excitement, grinned broadly as he approached her, swiftly rolling up the tablecloths and whatever utensils remained on them.

"Look out, Sis!" he called as he hurried past her. "You almost wound up in there with the forks and spoons!"

They dashed together onto the broad porch and into the kitchen, where Vera, the Bradleys' longtime housekeeper, directed the sudden rush of volunteers. "Willie," she cried, "I hear something clinking in those cloths. Don't you dare walk off and leave them all balled up in the corner that way."

"Yes, ma'am," Willie responded, giving her a cheeky grin and a wink as he moved to obey.

Lizzie set the bowls on the countertop, carefully removing the dishes and stacking them neatly next to the sink. Vera declined offers to help clean up and shooed everyone outside to continue visiting, giving Lizzie a sharp look when she went by.

The flush of excitement ebbed away, and Lizzie felt as listless as before. She joined the rest of her family and some of the ranch hands out on the porch. Eddies of conversation swirled around her as she passed by happily chattering clusters of people and stood alone at the end of the porch, her head resting against the corner post.

The much-awaited rain was coming down in earnest now, the large drops pelting the dusty ground as if eager to make up for their long absence. Lizzie closed her eyes and sniffed, enjoying the pungent smell of rain-dampened earth. Thunder rumbled in the distance, and the wind whipped some of the drops toward her, splashing her cheeks.

Instead of drawing away, she remained pressed against the post, enjoying the sensation of the wind tumbling her hair and tugging at her skirt. She squeezed her eyes shut even tighter, willing the wind to blow away the confusing thoughts that had beset her lately.

A tug on her arm roused her from her reverie. She looked down to see her cousin Rose, her face smudged and hair ribbons dangling limply. "Lizzie, aren't you listening? I've been talkin' and talkin', and you won't answer me."

"I'm sorry, Rose. I guess I was daydreaming."

"You must always be daydreaming anymore," the little girl complained. "Half the time when someone talks to you, you don't even hear 'em."

Stung by the justice of Rose's remark, Lizzie made an effort to pull herself together. She knelt in front of the eight-year-old. "I'm listening now," she assured her. "What's the trouble?"

Rose's lower lip jutted out belligerently. "It's Sammy," she said, referring to her twin brother. "He and Travis are being mean to me."

Lizzie tried to smother a smile. The squabbling of the three siblings was legendary. "You know who you and your brothers remind me of?" she asked. Rose shook her head solemnly. "You remind me of what Willie and I were like when we were your age."

Rose's eyes grew round with wonder. "You and Willie?" she asked suspiciously, as if doubting whether anyone who had reached the advanced age of nineteen could once have been eight years old herself.

Lizzie nodded emphatically. "We were either the best of friends or at each other's throat," she said. "Either way, it seemed like we were always getting into trouble."

"Willie's still in trouble a lot of the time," Rose said solemnly.

Lizzie managed a small smile. "Not as much as he used to be," she told her cousin. "And he's only sixteen. He's still growing up."

Rose eyed her gravely. "But you're all growed up, aren't you?" she asked. "You hardly ever get in trouble." She sighed. "I hope I grow up real fast, so I don't have any more problems."

Lizzie winced. How could she tell the little girl that growing up brought more problems than she ever dreamt of? She couldn't, she decided. She didn't even know specifically what her problems were — only the vague unsettled feeling she'd had lately that things were changing faster than she could keep up with them.

"Tell you what," she said, scrubbing at the little girl's cheek with her handkerchief. "Let's get your ribbons tied and your face and hands washed, then you can go back and play with Sam and Travis some more." When Rose seemed ready to protest, she added, "It really will get better someday. I promise. Boys go through stages like this."

"Okay," Rose agreed. She reached out to give Lizzie an enormous hug. "Thanks, Lizzie. I'll be glad when I'm grown and know all the right things to do, like you."

Like me? Lizzie watched the little girl scamper off and felt a wave of despair twist at her heart. *Honey, if you only knew! Half the time, I don't even feel like I know who I am anymore.*

Willie appeared at the front door and scanned the crowd on the porch until he spotted Lizzie. He made his way smoothly through the small knots of people, grinning and making lighthearted comments as he passed. He paused for a moment to give his aunt a hug and bent to peck a quick kiss on his mother's cheek. Both women shook their heads and smiled at him indulgently.

His lively blue eyes lit up when he reached Lizzie, showing a familiar mischievous twinkle. He lounged against the porch rail, trying his best to look nonchalant. "Have I got a great idea!" He spoke softly from the corner of his mouth. A slight frown crossed his face when Lizzie didn't respond immediately. "I said I've got a great idea, Sis — one of my best. Don't you want to know what it is?"

Lizzie stirred uneasily. Willie's "great

ideas" had gotten them into a ton of trouble during their growing-up years. Well, to be honest, she'd had just as many ornery ideas as Willie, maybe more. Only last summer, in fact, it had been her notion for them to sneak into the bunkhouse when the cowboys were absent and move all the mattresses up into the rafters. Now, though, the prospect of mischief didn't even begin to appeal to her.

"I don't think I feel up to pulling any pranks today, Willie."

Willie's brow furrowed. "What's the matter, Sis, you sick?"

"No, I'm not sick," she answered impatiently. Then, seeing his dejected look, she gave in. "Okay, what's your brilliant idea?"

Willie's face lit up. Casting a sidelong glance at the chattering crowd on the porch, he slid one hand under his vest and pulled out a stout stick that had been cut in half. One end of each piece had the point of a hat pin protruding from it.

"You know that new gray Stetson Bert's so proud of?" he asked, referring to the favorite headgear of one of the cowboys. Willie's eyes gleamed. "Well, all we have to do is stick these pins in his hat, one through each side, and it'll look like someone jammed the whole stick through.

It won't hurt the hat any, but Bert will have a fit!" He stopped, looking immensely proud of himself. "What do you think?" he asked.

A cold weight seemed to settle in Lizzie's stomach. "I don't think so, Willie. It just doesn't seem . . . right."

"Not right? What do you mean, not right?" Even Willie's crestfallen expression couldn't motivate her to give in and get involved, as it surely would have only a few months ago. She shrugged in irritation.

"It just seems . . . I don't know . . . childish, I guess. Go ahead if you want to. I just don't feel like doing it, that's all."

Willie's disappointment turned to vexation. "I don't get it, Lizzie. We've always done everything together. You've always been my best friend. But lately, you don't want to do anything but moon around all over the place. You go around like you're walking in your sleep, and you don't hear half the things people say to you. If you're not sick, then what's wrong with you?" He turned on his heel and stomped away in disgust.

Lizzie watched his retreating figure. "I don't know, Willie," she murmured softly. "I just don't know."

Returning to her previous position at the

post, she closed her eyes and let the breeze tug at her hair, savoring the welcome chill of the raindrops that made their way past the eaves to splatter on her skin.

From the opposite end of the porch, Adam McKenzie watched the loosened tendrils of hair play around Lizzie's face, feeling the familiar longing stir within him. *She looks like an angel,* he thought. *A dreamy, gray-eyed angel.*

Adam leaned back, bracing his hands against the porch railing. Charles and Jeff had declared this a ranch holiday, with only absolutely essential work to be done. Today he could take a guilt-free break and indulge himself in feasting his eyes on the most beautiful sight in northern New Mexico.

Lizzie swept a finger across one cheek, capturing a lock of golden hair and tucking it behind her ear. Adam wished he could caress that cheek, stroke that hair, whisper his feelings into that ear.

He swallowed, trying to dislodge the lump in his throat. Unable to do it, he cleared his throat loudly and turned resignedly toward the barn. No matter how pleasant the distractions, the horses still needed to be fed.

Chapter 2

"Mama! Lizzie's comin'!"

Lizzie heard Rose's shrill yell long before her horse reached the barn at her aunt and uncle's home. She rounded the corner of the building to see her little cousin skipping to meet her.

"Can I take Dancer, Lizzie? Can I tie him up for you?"

Lizzie dismounted with an easy grace born of countless hours in the saddle and had started to hand the reins to Rose when another high voice broke in.

"Don't you touch Dancer, Rosie! It's my turn!" An eight-year-old whirlwind with Rose's chestnut hair and blue eyes burst through the front door of the white frame house and into the yard.

"Is not!" Rose countered.

"Is too! You got him last time."

Lizzie tried to suppress a smile when Rose's eyes narrowed at her twin and her foot began tapping an ominous tattoo in the dust.

"Samuel Austin Bradley, you know that's not true," she accused. "Last time Lizzie was here, you got to brush Dancer and feed him and water him and everything, 'cause I was in the house helping Lizzie and Mama. You're just trying to sneak an extra turn."

Young Sam's eyes bulged, and he opened his mouth to make a hot retort. Lizzie decided she'd better step in before fists started flying.

"All right, Sam, that's enough," she said, trying to sound stern. "Rose is right. You did get to take care of Dancer last time, so it's her turn today." Noting his mutinous expression, she went on. "My saddle got awfully dusty on the ride over today. Do you think you could unsaddle Dancer and wipe it down for me?"

Sam puffed out his chest and answered, "Sure, Lizzie. I'll polish it up real nice!"

She watched the two walk away — Rose leading Dancer, Sam following along and keeping a proprietary eye on the saddle — with a sigh of relief, hoping the uneasy truce would last. Tapping on the partly open front door, she let herself in at Judith's call. "You saw?" she asked Judith, who was seated at the quilting frame near the large window.

Judith nodded. "And heard. That was a nice touch, making Sammy feel useful."

Lizzie sagged into a chair across from Judith. "Do they ever let up? How do you manage it?"

"Well, in addition to relying on a lot of prayer and the Lord's wisdom, I have one secret weapon."

Lizzie's eyes widened. "You do? What is it?"

Judith's eyes twinkled as she leaned toward Lizzie and lowered her voice conspiratorially. "I had a lot of prior experience with some rambunctious Bradley children," she confided.

Lizzie stared blankly for a moment, then felt her face redden when she realized her aunt was referring to her and her brother in their younger days.

"Oh, no!" she protested. "Willie and I may have been a handful, but we were never . . ." Her voice trailed off at Judith's look of amusement. "All right," she conceded. "I guess we were every bit as rowdy as those two."

"At least!" Judith laughed in remembrance. "If you weren't pretending to be outlaws plundering the West, you were plotting to nail the outhouse door shut. Sometimes I used to wonder what was more dangerous — a full-scale Indian raid or the two young Bradleys."

"But you did say it gave you experience," Lizzie reminded her with an impish grin.

"That's true," Judith replied. "So count your blessings, Lizzie." At the younger girl's puzzled expression, she continued, making an obvious effort to maintain a straight face. "The experience you're gaining now with Rose and Sam will be excellent training for you when you're trying to deal with your own children."

"My own?" Lizzie sputtered. "Oh, no. I'm not having any like *that!*" She clapped both hands across her mouth, appalled at what she had just said. Then, seeing one corner of her aunt's mouth twitch upward despite her best efforts, she amended sheepishly, "I guess I won't have much choice in the matter, will I? Is that one of those cases of 'sowing and reaping' do you think?"

"No doubt about it," Judith answered. Her tone was solemn, although her eyes sparkled with mischief. "Somewhere in the Bradley makeup is a strain of pure orneriness. The only consolation for those of us who have to deal with it is that it's sure to come back upon them when they become parents themselves. What do you think keeps me holding on with Sam and Rose?" she added mischievously.

A laugh welled up inside Lizzie and burst forth in a delighted gurgle. "So that's your secret? You can stand it now because you know they'll have to go through the same thing later?" Her aunt nodded, and both women burst into gales of laughter.

The front door opened and Sam strode into the room. "What's so funny?"

"Nothing, dear," Judith answered, wiping her eyes. "Just thinking ahead to the future."

"Oh," Sam said doubtfully. "Can I use some of those rags you cut up to clean Lizzie's saddle?" At his mother's nod, he left again, shaking his head over the mysteries of women.

Judith followed him with her gaze, smiling tolerantly. She rubbed her swollen belly, slowly tracing large circles with the flat of her hand.

"Are you all right?" Lizzie asked, concern coloring her voice.

"Fine," Judith reassured her, shifting to a more comfortable position. "I think all our silliness woke up the baby. He'd been resting quietly, but now he's awake and raring to go. Here," she said, reaching over to grasp Lizzie's hand and place it on her protruding abdomen. "See for yourself."

Startled, Lizzie stiffened for a moment, then relaxed. She could make out a solid form beneath the taut fabric of her aunt's dress. "That's the baby?" she whispered hesitantly.

"That's him," Judith affirmed. "Now just keep your hand still for a moment and see what happens."

Keeping her arm in position, Lizzie hooked one foot around the leg of her chair and scooted it closer to Judith's. She waited, trying not to move or make a sound. Her eyes widened as she felt the form shift beneath her hand. "He's moving," she breathed, just loud enough for her aunt to hear. "He's really moving!"

Judith smiled serenely. "Keep your hand right there. He's just getting started."

The movement ceased when she spoke, and Lizzie started to remove her hand. Judith stopped her with a quick shake of her head. Suddenly, rapid fluttering erupted beneath her palm. Judith grinned when Lizzie's gaze met hers in disbelief, then lowered again, watching the frenzied movements that were clearly visible.

"I can't believe it," Lizzie said in awe when the baby's performance had ended. "It felt like it might if I could put my hand in a pot of boiling water and feel the bubbles churning all around. But that felt a lot more solid than bubbles would!"

"It did, indeed!" Judith replied, laughing. "Here, let me show you what you were feeling." She moved her own hand across her abdomen, probing with her fingertips at intervals, then told Lizzie to place her own fingers on top of hers. "Press right there," she said, slipping her fingers out from underneath Lizzie's. "No, don't worry. You won't hurt me. Do you feel that hard, rounded spot?"

Utterly entranced, Lizzie could only nod. She moved her fingers gently back and forth, tracing the outline of the little lump beneath them.

"That's a knee," Judith told her. "And over here, I think . . . yes." She pressed against another spot. "Move your fingers over here. See if you can feel another hard spot, only smaller and sharper."

Lizzie complied, fascinated. She nodded when she located the tiny object her aunt had described. "What is it?"

"An elbow."

Lizzie noted the relative positions of the elbow and knee, then continued to probe, following the baby's outline. "Then that must be the back. And is that the head?"

She gasped and drew her hand away at the realization she had been shamelessly prodding her aunt's midsection. "Oh, I'm sorry! I didn't mean to get so carried away."

"Don't worry," Judith said, squeezing her hand. "I understand how fascinating it is. Here I am, getting ready for my fourth child, and I'm just as intrigued by it all now as I was the first time with the twins. Except," she reflected, "that the twins were twice as lively as this little fellow."

"You can't mean that!" Lizzie protested. "Why, it was one thing to feel him kick like that from the outside, but to have that going on *inside* you, then with two instead of just one . . ." Her voice trailed off and she shook her head. "I can't imagine it. Is it awful?"

"Awful? No, not at all. Even when my babies were kicking their hardest, it was a reassurance to me that they were strong and doing fine and a reminder of the precious mystery that was taking place." She took up her needle and leaned over the quilting frame as far as her protruding middle would allow. "Now let's get working on this quilt. I want to have it finished before the baby comes. If we don't, it'll be awhile before I'll be able to help you with it again."

In a daze, Lizzie moved her chair to the opposite side of the quilting frame and picked up one of the threaded needles Judith had prepared. Concentrating on taking tiny, even stitches across the bright colors of the Wedding Ring quilt helped steady her thoughts, but she couldn't help thinking again and again about the baby and the miracle taking place inside her aunt's body. To distract herself, she began talking.

"Do you really think Mama will like this quilt?"

"For the hundredth time, she'll be thrilled. She honestly doesn't know you've learned to quilt?" Judith shook her head in amazement. "It's a wonder you've managed to keep this a secret. Not too many secrets last around here."

"I think after she tried so hard to teach me to sew when I was younger and not at all interested, she finally gave up," Lizzie answered. "I was such a tomboy that all I cared about was spending time around the bunkhouse with Willie and the ranch hands and learning to ride. I pestered them half to death to teach me to rope, but I didn't care a lick about anything to do with a needle."

She reached the end of her thread, fastened it, and picked up another needle. "With Mama being such a lady and knowing how to do all the right things, I think it's been hard on her that I cared about so many of the wrong things and didn't care at all about the right ones."

Judith frowned. "What do you mean?"

Lizzie faltered, trying to find the right words. "I'm really not sure. It's just that I sometimes think she'd rather I was more like her instead of the way I am."

Judith stopped abruptly in midstitch. "Lizzie Bradley, do you think for one minute that your mother isn't proud of you?"

"Well, not that exactly, I guess." Lizzie squirmed uncomfortably, wishing she had not brought up this subject. "But she's so feminine and ladylike, and I'm so . . . so . . ." Words failed her, and she shook her head in frustration.

"What I started out to say was, thank you for teaching me how to quilt. When I finally realized how much it would mean to Mama for me to learn something like this, I thought it would be fun to surprise her, that's all. I really appreciate all the time you've taken, helping me with this." She kept on with her stitching, eyes focused determinedly on the bright pieces of fabric.

Judith still hadn't resumed stitching. "Honey," she said gently, her voice taking Lizzie back to earlier years when she had nestled happily on her aunt's comforting lap, "I want you to understand something."

Lizzie, stitching busily, made a sound to indicate that she was listening.

"Your mother and I have talked a lot about our growing-up years, about how both of us were brought up. I've only heard about the Virginia plantation where your mother was raised, but you've actually been there and seen it, haven't you?"

Lizzie nodded, memories of the large white house with its graceful verandahs and sweeping lawns springing into her mind. Her mother's upbringing had been suitable for a proper Southern young lady, and she apparently took to it with her usual style and grace. Lizzie knew she would never have been able to measure up to the standards her grandmother had set, nor would she have wanted to.

"It was a different world," Judith continued. "A world your mother fit into quite well but not the world she wanted to stay in."

Lizzie's head snapped up, her hands stilled for once, the beginnings of hope flaring up as she searched her aunt's face, trying to read the true meaning of her words.

"Your mother loved her parents, of course, and I know she appreciated all they did for her. But when your father came along, she was more than ready to make her life with him, in spite of their disapproval."

"Disapproval?" Lizzie echoed, her mind whirling. "They didn't like my father?"

"It wasn't so much that they disliked him, I think, as the fact that they felt she'd be marrying beneath her if she accepted his proposal."

Lizzie straightened indignantly, jabbing the point of her needle into one finger. She yelped and popped the throbbing finger into her mouth, trying to soothe the pain.

"I can't believe anyone could think that about my father," she said, mumbling around her finger. "Look at this ranch. Look at what he and Uncle Jeff have built here. Look at the time he spends in Santa Fe with all those politicians. Why, he's been there all this past week. People respect him and his opinions. He's an important man!" she finished indignantly. "How could they ever feel that way about him?"

Judith smiled gently. "When your

mother and father first met, he didn't have any of this," she reminded Lizzie. "He and his family still lived in Texas, and as far as your Virginia grandparents were concerned, he was just a shirttail relative visiting one of their neighbors. Your mother was the one who could see past the inexperienced youngster he was then to the fine man he could become."

Lizzie pulled the finger out of her mouth and inspected it, grimacing at the coppery taste of blood in her mouth. "Thank goodness for that!" she said tartly.

An all-too-familiar knot in her stomach made her forget the pain in her finger. "But after all those years out here, Mama's still such a lady. How can she not be disappointed in me?" Her throat tightened, and she lowered her gaze to the quilt once again, hoping her aunt hadn't seen the sudden tears that stung her eyes.

"What I'm trying to say, Lizzie, is that your mother sees not only the girl you are now but the woman you're becoming. She doesn't see you as failing to meet some standard your grandmother set. She sees you as a wonderful, unique person with a special life planned for her by the Lord. Watching that person unfold is an adventure not a disappointment."

Nothing broke the silence as the two women stitched steadily. Intent on keeping her lines straight and her stitches even, Lizzie found that one part of her mind was still free to ponder what her aunt had said.

If only it were true! As a child, she'd been much more interested in tomboyish activities than matters of propriety, but back then she hadn't cared what anyone else thought. At nineteen, the difference between her perception of herself and the accomplishments proper young ladies were supposed to have achieved was something she felt keenly.

She could hardly believe her lovely, well-brought-up mother could be satisfied having a daughter like her. But if Aunt Judith said it was so . . .

"It really is all a mystery, isn't it?" Lizzie asked abruptly.

"What is?"

"Oh, life and growing up and all. Sometimes I feel like your baby there." She flushed when Judith glanced up and raised her eyebrows questioningly, knowing she wasn't saying it the way she wanted to. "I mean, he's there inside you, a real, live person, with his own identity. But he's still developing and growing so he'll be ready to be born when the time comes. He's still

32

becoming the person he's supposed to be.

"That's kind of how I am," she went on, feeling that she was beginning to express some of what she felt. "I've lived for nineteen years now, and as far as the calendar's concerned, I'm an adult. But I don't feel like it. I think I'm still not finished. I'm growing and developing like your baby, trying to become the person I'm supposed to be. But I don't even know who that person is!" she ended in a wail.

"I look at other girls my age, girls I've known growing up. Most of them are already married. A couple of them are at finishing schools back east, and the rest at least have some sense of who they are. But me — all I am is confused!" She flung her hands out in frustration, connecting with a vase full of marigolds and pansies and knocking it to the floor with a crash.

She stared at the jagged crockery fragments and sodden petals. "Oh, Aunt Judith, I'm so sorry!" She knelt to pick up the broken pieces. "See what I mean? I'm just a mess!" The tears poured from her eyes in earnest, blurring her view of her aunt pushing herself to her feet and moving heavily into the next room. By the time she returned, Lizzie had disposed of the ruined vase, mopped up the soggy mess, and dried her eyes, although they felt puffy and swollen.

Judith carried a tray with two steaming cups and set it on a low table near the settee. Lowering herself slowly onto the seat, she patted the cushion next to her. "Come over here and have a cup of tea. It'll do wonders for you."

Lizzie complied, wiping her nose surreptitiously as she did so. Judith slipped one arm around her shoulders and pulled her close. "Listen to me, Elizabeth Bradley. There is nothing in the world wrong with you. God has a special timetable for each one of us, and you're no different. Quit worrying about what other girls your age are doing, and start concentrating on being the person He created *you* to be. You're on a voyage of discovery — enjoy it!" She gave Lizzie a squeeze and handed her one of the cups.

"Thanks, Aunt Judith." From the time Judith had come to be a part of the Bradley family, Lizzie had turned to her for refuge in times of confusion. For the first time in a long time, she felt like she might regain a sense of being acceptable. "I'm so glad you married Uncle Jeff," she blurted out impulsively.

"Well, so am I," her aunt replied, and

they both laughed. Lizzie tried to remember — didn't the Bible say something about laughter being good like a medicine? It seemed like today's dose had gone a long way toward helping to heal the way she'd been feeling lately.

She glanced at Judith with affection. "Was it like this with your aunt? The one you grew up with?"

Judith looked as though she didn't know whether to burst into laughter or tears. Then a resigned smile curved her lips. "You mean being able to talk things out like this?" She shook her head slowly. "No, it was nothing like this. When I went to live with my aunt, I was the same age you were when I came here. My mother had died not long before, and my aunt offered my father and me a home. He accepted, trying to do what was best for me, I suppose, and probably felt having a woman's influence would be good for me."

She stared into the distance for a moment, apparently lost in her memories. "Aunt Phoebe was nothing like my mother, even though they were sisters. I think she cared for me in her own way, but she wasn't a very demonstrative person. I was never able to take my problems or questions to her." She blinked, then seemed to return to the present and looked at Lizzie. "At one time, I felt terribly sorry for myself over the way she treated me. But now I can see how it all worked into God's plan."

Lizzie shook her head doubtfully. "Being treated badly was part of God's plan? How?"

"If I'd been comfortable and content back in St. Joseph, I never would have come out west to start a new life. And if I hadn't done that, I never would have met your uncle Jeff and become part of this wonderful family.

"You see?" she continued. "Those growing-up years were hard. They weren't what I wanted. But if I hadn't gone through them, I wouldn't have what I do now."

Lizzie nodded, trying to see things from this new perspective. "So maybe what I'm going through now will all work out in the long run?"

"Absolutely," her aunt said with conviction. "God promises that in His Word. The Lord is the *hope* of His people, Lizzie, remember that."

"Hope," Lizzie breathed. "That's exactly what I need." She gave her aunt a warm hug. "I'm sorry you didn't have a good life with your aunt, but I'm glad, too, since it brought you here." She drew back a bit in concern. "That sounds awful, doesn't it?"

Judith chuckled. "I know what you mean, and I couldn't agree more."

Lizzie hugged her again, relieved. "I'd better be getting back now. I'm sorry we didn't get more done on the quilt."

"Don't you worry," Judith said, smiling. "Sometimes more important things come up. Besides, we're close to being finished. Two or three more sessions ought to do it. Can you come again next week?"

"Maybe even before then," Lizzie assured her. "For now, though, I'd better get going and take Dancer for a good run before I go home. As far as Mama knows, I'm just out for my daily ride, and Dancer had better look like he's done more than stand in your barn munching hay."

With her aunt's reassuring words echoing in her mind, she guided the buckskin gelding in a wide loop on her way back to the ranch house.

Everything would work together for good, she reminded herself. Aunt Judith said so, and God Himself had promised it.

Chapter 3

When Lizzie led Dancer into the barn, she was delighted to see her father's big black stallion contentedly munching grain in his own stall. She unsaddled Dancer quickly, giving him a hurried but thorough grooming, and closed him in his stall with a full ration of oats.

Hurrying to the house, she paused to smooth her hair before she entered. Charles stood before the fireplace, where he was addressing Jeff, Abby, Willie, and Adam, who stood in the back of the room, leaning casually against the wall. Charles's face creased in a delighted grin when Lizzie entered, and he broke off in midsentence to sweep his daughter up in a bear hug. Lizzie returned his hearty squeeze and thought for the thousandth time how much she loved and admired her father.

"It's good to have you back," she told him. "I missed you."

Charles smiled affectionately and cupped her cheek in his hand. "I'm glad to be home, honey. It's good to have a part in territorial affairs, but it's even better to be back with my family."

"How was Santa Fe?" Lizzie took a seat on a footstool next to the chair where Willie sat. "Did I miss hearing all the news?"

"Hardly," her father replied. "I just got started."

"Actually," her uncle Jeff said dryly, "he started awhile ago, but he's just now working up a good head of steam."

Everyone laughed, including Charles. "All right," he said, looking a bit sheepish, "I'll admit I get a little worked up over all that's going on in the capital —"

"A little!" Jeff whispered loudly, winking broadly at Lizzie and Willie.

Charles shook his head in mock exasperation, cleared his throat, and began again. "As I was saying, the state of the territory is precarious, with all the trouble that's still going on down in Lincoln County," he said, referring to the conflict between two factions over contracts for military supplies that had escalated into bloody violence two summers earlier.

"I thought all that was over." Lizzie's

mother wore a worried frown.

"It was supposed to be," Charles replied grimly. "But things never settled down completely. Lately there have been more outbreaks of lawlessness — everything from small-time rustling to open raids on some of the outlying ranches."

"What about the law?" Abby asked. "Aren't they doing anything to stop it?"

Charles snorted. "A good number of the undesirables the Rangers ousted from Texas have made their way into the territory, and some of them have decided to give themselves the appearance of being law-abiding citizens by joining the posses. The very ones who are supposed to uphold the law are often no better than the ones they're chasing!

"Governor Wallace is doing his best to resolve the situation," he continued. "He's offered Billy the Kid a full pardon if he'll turn himself in. If that young killer will give himself up, maybe some of his gang will see the light and settle down. Short of that, I don't know what it will take to bring peace to New Mexico."

Lizzie looked around the room. Every face wore a grim expression, with the exception of Willie's.

"How can you say Billy's bad?" he

blurted out. "Haven't you heard the story about how he rode all night to get medicine for that little Mexican girl? She almost died! She *would* have died, too, if Billy hadn't done that."

As the company gaped at him, Willie leaned forward in his seat, warming to his subject. "Folks talk about the people he's killed. Well, maybe he has killed some. But it's only been to defend himself or protect someone else. Billy and his friends are more like knights than outlaws. It's all been blown up bigger than it really is!"

Jeff spoke softly. "Better get all your facts straight, boy, before you go taking someone's part."

Willie opened his mouth to protest, but at a stern glance from his father, he slumped back in his chair, a look of disgust on his face.

Lizzie studied her brother out of the corner of her eye. Surely he couldn't be defending that notorious killer! Willie might be fun-loving, even ornery at times, but there wasn't a truly mean bone in his body. She turned her attention back to the group listening to Charles.

"There's grave concern among those in the territorial government that this will have an adverse effect on our hopes for

41

statehood," he said. "If we can't manage our own affairs successfully, why should they admit us into the Union?"

Jeff's brow furrowed in concern at his brother's words. "We've come too far to have all our hard work destroyed now."

Abby's gaze searched her husband's face. "Aside from the effect it may have on the statehood issue, will the trouble stay in Lincoln County? You don't think it will affect us here, do you, Charles?"

Charles's gaze softened, and he regarded his wife tenderly. "I hope not, Abby. I truly hope not. It's a hard thing to have put in so many years of effort, only to have all our work placed into jeopardy by the actions of a few desperadoes."

Lizzie crossed her arms and hugged herself tightly. *Please, God, don't let the trouble spread here.* There had been so little unrest at the ranch in all the years they'd been there that the idea of something like this rocking her secure world was unthinkable.

Next to her, Willie stirred. "I don't believe they're desperadoes," he declared hotly. "But even if it's true, maybe if they came up here, we'd have some excitement for a change!" He stood and stalked out of the room, slamming the door behind him.

Silence gripped the room as the group stared after him in shock. Charles recovered first. "What in the world has gotten into that boy?" he demanded.

Adam straightened from his place in the back of the room. "I remember how restless I was when I was his age. I wanted to lick the world and had no doubt I could do it. A boy that age needs heroes, but Willie's picking some bad ones if he's looking up to the likes of that crew."

Lizzie started at the sound of Adam's voice. He had stood so still and been so quiet, she had forgotten he was even in the room. It had always been that way, though, she reflected. She heard other girls giggling over his brawny physique, the sandy hair that would never quite stay in place, and his dark brown eyes. But for her, Adam had been a part of the place for so long that he seemed a natural part of the background — like the furniture, the wallpaper, or the scenery outside.

She watched her father glower at the closed door as though he could see Willie right through it. Then he exchanged a troubled glance with her mother. "They all have their growing pains, I guess. I hope that's all this is." He turned his head and smiled at his daughter. "At least we've never had a reason to worry about Lizzie."

Lizzie flushed with surprised pleasure at the general murmur of agreement from the others. Had they always felt like this? she wondered. And if they had, why hadn't she realized it before now? The glow she felt at her family's approval dimmed a bit when she remembered Willie's uncharacteristic attitude.

She must remember to pray for Willie, she decided. Maybe he was going through the same type of uncertainty she had been experiencing. She would pray that God would work things out according to His will in Willie's life, too.

Chapter 4

Lizzie walked toward the barn, the glory of the bright summer day matching her light-hearted mood. Life always seemed more unsettled when her father was gone on business. Having him home again the past week made her feel that the pieces of her life were back in their proper places.

Small clouds like white puffballs floated in scattered clumps across the sky, but she knew they would soon begin gathering, massing into thunderheads that would bring the afternoon rains. Lizzie loved the feeling of anticipation that came before a rain and looked forward to her daily ride, knowing Dancer would be as eager as she was to work off excess energy before the storm broke.

Far off to the west, a rider appeared as a dot on the horizon. One of the cowboys heading in for some reason, she supposed. Nearer at hand, Bert was mending a hinge on the corral gate, and Hank prepared to mount a green-broke horse in the breaking pen.

Even though she had lived on a ranch all her life, the process of breaking a horse to ride — that contest of wills between man and animal — still fascinated Lizzie. She slowed her pace, her attention riveted on the drama about to take place.

The horse, a rawboned dun, stood stiff-legged, ears laid back flat against his head. Hank stroked the horse's neck and spoke in a soothing tone. Lizzie respected the way Hank treated the green horses, trying to win their confidence instead of attempting to master them by brute force. The dun snorted nervously, and Lizzie could see the muscles bunch in his neck.

Hank carefully placed his foot into the left stirrup and swung smoothly into the saddle. The horse's nostrils flared when he felt a man's weight on his back for the first time. His eyes flared wide now; Lizzie could see a ring of white around each dark iris.

Hank sat easy in the saddle. He looked completely relaxed, but Lizzie knew he was on the alert, ready for a blowup.

It came without warning. With a shrill squeal of rage, the horse exploded into motion, like a spring compressed to its limit, then released. Leaping and twisting, he slashed the air with his forefeet, then lowered his head and thrust his hind feet high above him. Hank hung on gamely, shifting his weight to maintain his balance on the frantic animal's back.

Bert trotted over from the corral and stood on the lower rail of the breaking-pen fence. "Ride him, Hank!" he shouted. Dangerous as it was, this raw action never failed to thrill Lizzie. She moved closer to the pen, her eyes never leaving the spectacle.

"He has a lot of spirit, doesn't he?" she said quietly.

"That's for sure," Bert answered eagerly. "Look at him — full of fire and vinegar! He'll make a good cow pony when Hank's finished with him. Plenty of stamina in that one."

Hank's skillful handling seemed to be having the desired effect. The horse no longer lunged with his original violent force, and Hank was smiling, apparently confident the battle was nearly over.

The dun stopped abruptly in the center of the pen, head down and breathing hard. Hank, still wary, relaxed a bit. As if he had been waiting for that very response, the horse burst into action again, with all of his former determination.

Caught off guard, Hank was thrown slightly off center. Encouraged, the horse redoubled its efforts. Hank hung on grimly, although each jarring landing knocked him further off balance.

"Don't let him throw you, Hank!" Bert yelled. Lizzie held her breath, knowing a fall was inevitable.

The dun gave a mighty leap and twisted in the air. Hank threw himself as far from the pounding hooves as he could, landing hard. He lay still. Lizzie felt her heart pound heavily in her chest as she willed Hank to move. The horse, free of his load, ran toward the fallen cowboy, snorting vengefully.

"Get up, Hank! Get up!" Lizzie shrieked, aware that Bert was vaulting over the top rail even as she shouted.

Hank raised himself on his elbows and started to rise. His face twisted in pain and he sank back to the dust. Keeping watch on the raging animal, he began dragging himself away, using his arms to propel himself toward the edge of the pen and safety.

The horse whirled and glared at Bert, who skidded to a halt midway between the dun and Hank. Lizzie raced around the outside of the pen and dove under the fence near Hank. "Come on!" she screamed. She grabbed Hank under his arms and pulled for all she was worth. "You've got to get out of here before he kills you!"

"I think my leg's broke," Hank ground out through clenched teeth. He dug the toe of one boot into the ground and thrust himself forward. "I'll make it okay, but you'd better get back under that fence before you get hurt."

Lizzie continued to tug Hank toward the fence, an impossible distance away. Bert stood frozen, looking for an opportunity to gain control of the enraged animal.

Out of the corner of her eye, Lizzie saw Adam appear in the doorway of the barn, holding a partially mended bridle. "What's going on, Hank? Can't you keep your seat in that saddle?" he called cheerfully. Then he spotted Hank's prone figure, and his smile disappeared.

Dropping the bridle, he backed through the doorway again and reappeared with a lariat in his hand. "Easy, Bert," he called softly. "Don't make a sudden move and spook him."

"I'm not plannin' on movin' much at all," the cowboy replied. "Not until the situation changes a mite, anyway."

"Lizzie?" Adam's voice was sharp with concern. "You and Hank freeze, too. Let me ease over there and get a loop on him."

Knowing Adam's skill with horses, Lizzie obeyed without question. Hank, too, ceased his struggle to reach the fence.

Lizzie's breath stilled while she watched Adam approach the breaking pen, shifting his weight from one foot to the other and advancing so gradually he hardly seemed to move at all. "Easy, boy," he said in a calm, low voice. "Settle down, fella." In the same soothing tone and without raising his voice, he said, "As soon as I get this loop over his head, all of you get out of there in a hurry."

The dun's nostrils flared as he evaluated this new threat. His front hooves beat a nervous rhythm on the hard-packed earth, and his ears flicked back and forth as he tried to concentrate on all four humans at once.

Without warning, he pivoted on his hind legs and rushed madly toward Lizzie and Hank. Lizzie heard Adam's hoarse cry as she flung herself toward the fence and wriggled under the bottom rail. She could feel the vibration of the horse's pounding hooves.

Rolling over quickly, she saw Adam's muscular arm whirl and straighten, flinging the loop toward the horse's head. The dun swerved abruptly just as Adam released the rope, avoiding the noose by a fraction of an inch.

Adam immediately began to retrieve his rope for another try. Bert made his way out the other side of the pen and headed for his lasso. Only Hank was left inside with the infuriated animal.

Before Adam could prepare for another throw, the dun turned and headed for the side of the pen at breakneck speed. With a powerful thrust of his haunches, he cleared the top rail and bolted away.

Bert threw down his rope in disgust. "That's going to be one tough horse to catch again," he muttered.

Lizzie and Adam ran to Hank's side. "That was close," Hank said, grinning weakly. "I thought I was a goner there, for a minute."

"How bad are you hurt?" Adam asked.

"It's his leg. It may be broken," Lizzie told him. She raised her eyes to look at Adam and was stunned by the intensity of his gaze when it locked onto hers.

"And you! What did you think you were doing?" he demanded.

Lizzie blinked and lowered her gaze before the force of his glare. Then she bristled. What right did he have to speak to her this way?

She opened her mouth to make a sharp retort, but a whoop from Bert interrupted her.

"Look! Look at that! I never seen anything like it!" Bert stared, mouth agape, at the scene unfolding to the west.

The rider Lizzie had seen earlier set his horse on a course that intercepted the escaping dun. When the dun swerved to evade him, the rider spurred his mount, gaining on the runaway with incredible speed. A thin line snaked out from the rider's hand and a loop settled gently around the dun's neck. Rather than jerking the animal to a stop, the rider gradually guided him in a wide arc back toward the waiting group.

Hank's strained voice broke the awed silence. "If it ain't too much bother . . ."

Lizzie started guiltily. "Oh, Hank, you poor thing!" She knelt beside the injured man. Adam hunkered down across from her.

Adam scanned the cowboy's leg. "I'm afraid you're right, Hank. Legs don't bend quite like that on their own. I'll get Bert to help me, and we'll get you inside and send for the doctor. Bert!" he called.

Bert tore his gaze from the advancing rider and hurried to help move Hank. "Did you see that?" he sputtered, bending over his injured friend. "Beats anything I ever did see. Why, I didn't know anyone could rope like that."

His voice trailed off as he and Adam disappeared inside the bunkhouse, carrying Hank between them. Lizzie watched them, anxiety for Hank clouding her excitement. The sound of approaching hoofbeats caught her attention, and she turned to greet their unexpected champion.

The man on horseback guided his mount to the breaking pen, where he opened the gate without dismounting, swung it wide, and shooed the recalcitrant bronc inside. Securing the gate, he rode back toward Lizzie and tipped his hat courteously.

He was, Lizzie judged, about twenty years old, with dark brown hair framing a narrow face. Deep-set eyes flashed a dazzling blue gleam her way, and he gave her a winning smile. "Tom Mallory at your service, miss."

Lizzie, suddenly aware she was gaping at the stranger like a codfish, tried to recapture some semblance of dignity. "Welcome to the Double B, Mr. Mallory, and thank you for your help. We're in your debt."

Tom Mallory leaned forward in his saddle. "Well, miss, I'll certainly keep that in mind."

Lizzie felt a furious blush heat her cheeks. What on earth was wrong with her? She had been around cowboys and ranch hands all her life, and none of them had ever affected her this way.

"If you'll excuse me, I'll go get my father," she said, trying not to sound as flustered as she felt. "I know he'll want to thank you himself, and I need to let him know one of the men needs a doctor." She turned toward the house, willing herself not to give in to her desire to break into headlong flight.

After checking on Hank and summoning the doctor, Charles strode over to the newcomer and held out his hand. "Mallory, I'm obliged. I understand you made a pretty impressive showing out there." He swept his hand toward the range.

Standing at her father's elbow, Lizzie couldn't seem to focus her eyes on anything but Tom Mallory. He was of medium height, smaller than her father, with the slender build and narrow hips of a rider. She took in the long, tapering fingers that gripped the belt of his chaps.

When he grinned boyishly at Charles, she saw how the cleft in his chin deepened. An unfamiliar tingling sensation began in her stomach and spread outward in a warm glow. What in the world was she doing, noticing so many details, and why were they affecting her this way? She clasped her hands in front of her, hoping no one would notice their trembling, and tried to concentrate on the men's conversation.

". . . really wasn't much," Tom was saying. "Glad I could help out. I was riding in this way to see if there were any jobs open. Are you hiring?"

Charles beamed at him. "If you're looking for a job, it's yours. Hank will be laid up for a good while with that broken leg, and if I needed a recommendation, your actions out there tell me all I need to know about your qualifications. Put your gear in the bunkhouse and tell my brother, Jeff, you've signed on." He turned to introduce Lizzie. "This is my daughter," he began.

Tom Mallory swept his Stetson from his head with a flourish. "I've already had the pleasure," he said. He turned the full force of his dazzling blue eyes on Lizzie, and she felt as though she'd been struck by a thunderbolt.

"We're pleased to have you with us, Mr. Mallory," she managed.

"I'm honored, miss," he replied. Lizzie followed him with her gaze as he shouldered his bedroll and headed toward the bunkhouse.

Inside the bunkhouse, Willie sat helping Adam plait reins when Tom strode in. Tom stopped, taking a casual stance in the doorway.

"Where do I put my gear?" he asked.

Adam nodded toward a bunk in the corner. "Over there." He turned back to his leather work.

Willie dropped his end of the reins and moved ahead of Tom to sweep some tack off the bunk. "Glad to have you on board," he said, beaming.

Tom smiled in acknowledgment and set his belongings down on the bunk.

"Bert told me what you did out there," Willie continued. "He said he'd never seen anything like it. I guess it was really something, wasn't it, Adam?" Adam grunted noncommittally, holding the dangling ends of the reins Willie had dropped.

"It wasn't much," Tom responded. "Glad I could help."

"Wasn't much! Why, you should hear Bert tell about the way you rode that horse and threw that rope! Where'd you learn that, anyway?"

Tom's eyes crinkled at the corners as he grinned at Willie. "Oh, I've been around a bit, that's all."

"I'd sure like to learn how to do that," Willie hinted.

Tom clapped him on the shoulder and started for the door. "We'll see what happens. I'd better tend to my horse now and make sure he's fed." He strode in the direction of the barn.

"Isn't he something?" Willie's eyes glowed with delight. "What do you think, Adam? Maybe I can learn some things from him while he's here. Do you think he'll have time to teach me?" Without waiting for an answer, he hurried out the door in pursuit of his newfound hero.

Adam exchanged a wry glance with Hank. "So what do you think of your replacement?" Adam asked the older man.

"I didn't exactly get a good view of all the goings-on," Hank replied dryly, "being face down in the dirt and all. But it sounds like he's 'really something,' " he added, mimicking Willie's unconcealed admiration.

Adam snorted. "Sounds like it, doesn't it?" He frowned when he saw Hank wince. "How bad's the leg?"

"Not so bad if I lie still." Hank shifted slightly on the bed, trying to get comfortable. "Talking helps keep my mind off it some." He watched Adam toss the unfinished reins down in disgust. "What's the matter? You look worried. Do you know Mallory from somewhere?"

Adam shook his head, annoyed with himself for not hiding his feelings better. "Nothing's wrong, Hank. At least, nothing I can put my finger on. I just feel uneasy. I don't really know why."

"It wouldn't have anything to do with him being the big hero instead of you, would it?" Hank chuckled when Adam gave him a hard stare.

"What's that supposed to mean?" Adam demanded.

"Oh, nothing much," Hank answered with an air of innocence. "Just that it must be awful hard to have them big gray eyes staring at this Mallory fellow instead of you."

"It's not like they stare at me all that

often," Adam muttered. He felt a surge of alarm knot up inside his stomach. Just how much had Hank guessed? And if Hank could read his feelings as easily as that, how many other people knew?

"It's nothing real obvious," Hank said, as if reading Adam's mind. "I just happen to be what you'd call observant. I had three brothers, and whenever one of them got love struck, he had the same hangdog expression on his face you have on yours whenever a certain young lady comes into view."

"You're imagining things," Adam said, trying to sound casual. "You better just lie still until the doctor gets here."

Hank snorted and gave Adam a knowing look but kept quiet.

Adam walked to the door of the bunkhouse. Fifty yards away, he could see Lizzie seating herself gracefully on the porch swing. He leaned against the door frame, watching her push herself gently back and forth with one dainty foot. His lips curved into a smile. Her hair gleamed like gold in the sunlight, even at this distance.

Adam was too far away to see her eyes, but he was fully aware of their gray depths. When he was a small boy, his father once took him to the Atlantic Ocean. Adam still remembered the swelling gray waves, exactly the same shade as Lizzie's eyes. *A man could drown in those eyes,* he thought. *And it wouldn't be a bad way to go.*

A quick movement off to one side caught Adam's attention, and he turned to see Tom Mallory standing at the corner of the corral, staring intently at Lizzie. *That's a hungry look if ever I saw one.* Adam's mouth hardened into a thin line. *The look of a coyote watching a defenseless rabbit. Or would I resent any good-looking man looking at Lizzie?*

Willie wheeled around the corner of the bunkhouse, nearly colliding with Adam. "Tom's going to teach me to rope," he announced, skidding to a stop. "Do you want to come, too, Adam? Maybe you can pick up a thing or two."

Adam clenched his teeth together hard enough to hear them grate. "Not today, Willie. I've spent too much time working on those reins already. I'm heading out."

He turned on his heel and went to saddle his horse.

Chapter 5

Three days later, Adam stood before the door of Charles Bradley's office. He took a deep breath to calm himself, realizing he was on edge after several nights with little sleep.

The advent of Tom Mallory at the Double B had been met with mixed responses. Charles and Jeff both appeared to be relieved to have a capable hand turn up just when Hank was injured and seemed pleased with Tom's ability. Hank watched Tom and Adam carefully in the bunkhouse but didn't share his thoughts with anyone, as far as Adam knew.

Willie had a full-fledged case of hero worship, spending as much time with Tom as he could manage and turning every conversation into a discussion of what Tom had said or done that day and what Willie learned from him.

And Lizzie . . . Adam's eyes clouded, remembering how often she had shown up unexpectedly around the corrals the last few days. If Tom wasn't there, she sighed and got ready for her daily ride without further dallying.

Adam shook his head helplessly. His own reaction had been to ignore the feelings churning inside him during the day and spend the night hours in a futile effort to sort out his thoughts. Tom Mallory awoke a response in him he had never experienced before. As he told Hank, there was no specific thing he could point to, nothing he could pin down. He just didn't trust the man. Or was it simply a case of out-and-out jealousy? He honestly didn't know. Maybe it was his own perceptions he didn't trust.

All this speculation didn't get the job done, he knew. He had set his course and he needed to follow it. He raised his hand and knocked on the heavy door.

"Come in," Charles called.

Pushing the door open, Adam saw both Charles and Jeff seated at the massive oak desk, studying a map of the Double B and the surrounding area.

"Do you have a minute?" Adam asked.

"We can always make time for you," Charles answered with a smile.

Jeff stood and stretched. "It's about time

someone rescued me. I was stiffening up, sitting and listening to all the plans my brother has," he said, grinning. "Do you want to talk to both of us or just Charles?"

"Both of you, if you have the time," Adam said. "I have some ideas, and I'd like to get your reactions, too."

"More plans, huh?" Jeff shook his head in mock despair. "Looks like I'm outnumbered today."

Adam grinned, relaxing for the first time in days. Both Bradley brothers were men he respected, and he valued the advice they'd given him in the past. He felt he'd earned a measure of respect from them in the years he had worked for them.

"I'm glad you have that map out," he began. "I wanted to ask your opinion on a piece of property."

"Really?" Charles raised his eyebrows in pleased surprise. "You're ready to get started on your own place?"

"That's what you get for being gone from the ranch so much," Jeff said, teasing his brother. "Adam's made a lot of progress over the last few months."

Adam felt a warm glow of pleasure. To have the support of these two men meant a great deal to him. He walked over to the desk and pointed to an area on the map. "I know you're familiar with the Blair place." He traced the property adjacent to the Double B with a work-hardened finger.

"Of course," Charles replied. "Wait a minute. Is old Thad putting it up for sale?"

Adam nodded. "He says he's getting along in years, and he wants to take what he's made and spend the time he has left with his sister in Denver. Personally, I think he wants company more than anything."

"Ranching isn't an easy way to make a living," Charles agreed, "and it's got to be hard not to have a family to share both the good and the bad times with.

"But," he continued, his eyes sparkling, "you're just a young fellow getting started. By the time you get the place built up a little, you ought to be the most eligible bachelor in these parts." He chuckled when Adam's face reddened. "He's sure come a long way from that scrawny kid who came out of nowhere all those years ago, hasn't he, Jeff?"

"I'll say," his brother agreed, settling himself on a corner of the desk. "You looked like a strong wind would blow you away back then. How long has it been, anyway? Eight years? Ten?"

"Ten years next spring," Adam confirmed. "I was only fifteen, and as wet behind the ears as any newborn foal. The only things I knew were how to work with horses and that I wanted to see the West."

"It took a lot of gumption, a youngster coming out on his own like that, with no family to fall back on," Jeff said.

"Wasn't much family left," Adam reminded him. "My folks were gone, and the owner of the horse place where my dad had been head trainer didn't have any use for a young pup like me. My older sister had married, and there wasn't much reason for me to stay around. All I ever wanted to do was have my own place where I could raise some good stock. Now it looks like that's going to happen, but it wouldn't have without your help."

"Don't take credit away from yourself," Charles said. "You've worked hard for us here, and you've earned every bit of what you have."

"Not everyone would have been willing for me to build my own corrals on their range and take time off to catch wild horses to break and sell."

"Which you've turned into some of the finest stock in the territory and which we're able to buy at a cut rate," Charles put in with a smile.

"If I can interrupt the meeting of this mutual admiration society," Jeff said, "what do you say we fine, noble souls listen to whatever it is this upstanding young fellow has to say?"

Charles laughed out loud, and Adam grinned self-consciously. It wasn't often he opened himself up to others this way, and he hoped he hadn't overstepped any boundaries. He enjoyed the good-natured banter between the brothers and appreciated them treating him as an equal.

Adam directed their attention to the map once again, telling them the asking price of the property and outlining his plans to set up his own horse ranch. He pointed out future locations of catch pens, breaking pens, and hay barns, his voice growing increasingly animated.

"So what do you think?" he asked at length. "Is this as good a proposition as I think it is, or have I just talked myself into something because I want it so much?"

The two brothers were silent for a moment. "Let's hear from Jeff first," Charles suggested.

Jeff cleared his throat. "The price is fair, so if you've got enough saved up, that's not a problem. The location is prime, and your ideas for setting things up sound like

you've put a lot of thought into them."
Adam nodded in wholehearted agreement.
No one else knew how many hours he had
spent planning the operation down to the
last detail.

"To be honest, I can't see a thing wrong
with it," Jeff concluded. "What about you,
Charles?"

"I'd have to agree," his brother said.
"For what you're planning, I can't think
of any place around here that would be
more suitable. Everything about it sounds
ideal. I think you're getting yourself a
setup with a lot of potential, Adam. Congratulations."

Adam's shoulders slumped in relief.
He'd thought long and hard about taking
this step and had hoped he'd covered all
the angles. Hearing such enthusiastic support from the Bradleys confirmed that his
ideas were sound. He took a deep breath
and let it out slowly, facing the idea that
soon he'd be his own boss, running his
own spread.

Charles heard his sigh and chuckled.
"Need a little fresh air? Let's move on out
to the porch.

"You know," he continued when they
were positioned comfortably against the
porch railing, enjoying the sweet summer

air, "the location is ideal in more ways than one."

Adam looked at him with a questioning frown.

"It borders the Double B," Charles explained, "which means you'll still be close by. It's selfish of me, I guess, but I'd hate to see you move out of the area. You're practically part of the family, you know."

Adam shifted uncomfortably, hoping Charles couldn't read his mind as well as Hank had.

"Last time I was over at the Blair place," Jeff said, "the buildings all looked like they were in pretty fair shape. Have you taken a good look at them?"

"I went over all of them," Adam said. "Everything's solid — the house, barn, outbuildings, corrals. Old Thad has really done a good job of keeping the place up. The only thing I'd change," he said, his eyes focusing on a point in the distance, "is the house. It's a little on the small side. I thought I'd enlarge it pretty soon or maybe build a new one."

The brothers exchanged curious glances. "I remember Thad's house pretty well," Charles said. "It's no mansion, but it seems to me there was plenty of room for one person." He nudged Adam with his elbow. "Do you have plans we don't know about?"

Adam hated the way he turned a bright red when he became flustered, and he could tell by the way the heat flushed over his face that it was happening right now. The gleeful grins of the brothers confirmed it.

"It was just a thought," he muttered. "Nothing to get excited about."

The front door closed, and all three men turned their heads to see Lizzie heading toward the porch steps, dressed for her ride. Her lustrous hair was caught in a braid that hung down her back, and Adam knew that if she came closer, he'd catch the scent of the rose water she always wore.

"Hello, Papa. Hello, Uncle Jeff," she called brightly. The two men voiced their greetings.

"Afternoon, Lizzie." Adam tipped his hat as he spoke.

She gave him a brief smile and a nod before she descended the steps.

Adam watched her walk away, noting her free, swinging gait and the sway of her heavy braid.

As Lizzie neared the barn, Tom Mallory appeared in the doorway. Adam watched as she looked up, apparently startled to see him, and spoke. He saw Tom flash a smile at her and move aside so she could enter the barn, then turn and follow her inside.

Adam knew his jealousy of Tom Mallory was unreasonable. He didn't have any outward claim to Lizzie, only the inner commitment of his heart. He'd never spoken of his feelings for Lizzie to her or anyone else; he couldn't, until he had a home to offer her — a home far better than a mere cowhand could afford. That, however, didn't prevent the feeling that a strong hand had reached into his stomach and given it a twist. He mumbled an excuse to the Bradleys and strode to the bunkhouse before they could see his dark expression.

Lizzie gave a little jump when Tom's lean frame appeared, blocking the doorway to the barn. Flustered, she gave a little laugh, hoping to cover her embarrassment.

Tom's bright blue gaze seemed to shoot right through her, and if that wasn't enough to unnerve her, he followed it up with a smile that seemed to be meant just for her. He moved aside just enough to let her pass, but not so far that she couldn't feel the spark that passed between them. Instead of going out to the corral as she expected, he turned and followed her inside.

Lizzie, who spent much of her life in that very barn, looked around her as though at a totally unfamiliar place. She pressed a hand against her stomach, trying to calm the fluttering that began the moment she walked past Tom. Glancing nervously in his direction, she saw he still stood there, watching her with an enigmatic smile.

"I–I'm just going to get my horse," she stammered, hating the way her voice quavered. She turned and started toward Dancer's stall, both relieved and disappointed when Tom didn't follow.

Slipping the bridle over Dancer's head, Lizzie paused a moment with her arms around the gelding's neck and pressed her face against his warmth. Here, the familiar smell of horse, straw, and grain soothed her jangled nerves, and she breathed deeply to steady herself.

When she led Dancer back down the aisle, Tom was waiting, lounging against the wall. And when she tied Dancer and started to brush him, Tom grabbed another brush and began working on the other side. Lizzie swallowed and tried to maintain her composure. What was it about Tom that made his nearness so unsettling?

Lizzie turned to reach for Dancer's

saddle blanket, but Tom moved past her and got to the rack first. "This one?" His eyes twinkled.

Lizzie nodded dumbly. Tom settled the blanket on Dancer's back, adjusting it for the horse's comfort, then turned back to Lizzie. "Which saddle is yours?" he asked. Lizzie pointed and watched him swing it smoothly into place, wondering at the constriction in her chest.

Finding her voice at last, Lizzie stepped forward and took hold of the cinch strap. "Thank you, but I've been doing this for most of my life," she said. "I really don't need any help." Her fingers responded like blocks of wood when she tried to thread the strap through the cinch ring, refusing to respond with their usual competence. She ground her teeth, wishing with all her heart that she didn't feel like a gawky twelve-year-old every time this man came near.

Tom smiled and stepped back, seeming to take no offense. He hooked his thumbs in his pockets and watched quietly while Lizzie completed her preparations. She gave Dancer's glossy black mane a final brush, adjusted the bridle, and checked the cinch once more because Dancer had a habit of puffing up when he was first saddled.

Lizzie grasped the reins under Dancer's chin and turned to lead him outside. Tom stepped back slightly, but not enough to allow her to pass without practically brushing against him. Lizzie timidly tilted her chin to look up at him, feeling spots of color rise in her cheeks when he held her gaze. They stood there, not moving, as though the moment were frozen in time.

Lizzie was vaguely aware of footsteps sounding on the doorstep. The steps paused, stopped. Then the door slammed shut with a crash, jolting her out of her trance. She sprang forward, dragging Dancer, and Tom's amused gaze.

Bert swung open the door, which now hung slightly out of kilter. "What'd you say to Adam, Lizzie?" he asked.

"N–nothing," she stammered, feeling her cheeks flame. "I didn't say a word."

Bert stared back over his shoulder across the corrals. "Wonder what got into him, then. He slammed the door and took off looking like a thundercloud."

"I really have no idea," Lizzie murmured. She hurriedly led Dancer from the barn, mounted, and set off, with Tom's low chuckle echoing in her ears.

Chapter 6

The recent rains settled the dust and lent a clean freshness to the air. Lizzie breathed deeply, savoring the scent of grass, sage, and cedar. Little by little, she felt as though she were regaining her equilibrium. She closed her eyes, simply enjoying the sensation of moving as one with Dancer's rolling gait.

Opening her eyes, she took in the vast landscape that had surrounded her for most of her life. To some, she supposed, the open grassland and cedar-studded hills punctuated by mountains in the distance might seem lonely, even barren. But Lizzie saw only the beauty, the wide expanse inviting her to measure up to her surroundings.

It was a perfect summer day. Heavy white clouds cast purple shadows, shielding her from the sun's heat. A light breeze stirred, bending the heads of the grasses. *Lord, when You created this land,*

You made it a very special place. Thank You for putting me here.

Her thoughts turned to a verse she read that morning. Ever since her conversation with Judith, Lizzie tried to spend time each day reading her Bible, instead of being satisfied with her typically sporadic efforts. If God had plans for her life, she reasoned, surely she should make an effort to know more about Him and His wonderful promises.

She began reading the book of Psalms. Remembering the book was supposed to contain a great many promises, she decided it would be the perfect place to begin her search. That morning, the fourth verse of Psalm 37 fairly leaped off the page. "Delight thyself also in the Lord; and he shall give thee the desires of thine heart." She caught her breath even now at the memory of how the words seemed to have been intended just for her.

Lord, You really do care about me, don't You? She hugged the precious knowledge to herself with a sense of wonder. It was easy to break into conversation with the Lord out here, away from the bustle of the ranch headquarters.

Tentatively she began again, speaking aloud this time. "Father, I really need to know what You think about my feelings for Tom. When I'm around him, he makes me feel special. Nervous, maybe, but special, too.

"I look at how Mama and Papa love each other and love You. Uncle Jeff and Aunt Judith are the same way. That's the kind of marriage I want to have, with someone who will love me like that."

She reined Dancer to the right to avoid some prairie dog holes, knowing the area beneath them would be honeycombed with tunnels and could cave in under Dancer's weight. The holes, she reflected, were like a sign pointing out an area of possible danger. *That's what I need from God. Something to show me which way is safe and where the danger lies.*

"Lord," she prayed, "You said You'd direct my paths. I need You to show me the right path now. The feelings I have for Tom feel so natural, so right. If he truly is the one You've chosen for me, then show me. Show my family, show Tom, show *everyone* that this is Your will. In Jesus' name, amen."

Feeling a renewed sense of hope, Lizzie touched Dancer's sides lightly with her heels, and the buckskin loped across the range. The wind whipped at her face, blowing away the clouds of confusion and doubt and leaving peace in their place.

The sun emerged from behind the clouds, and Lizzie, her eyes dazzled by the sudden brilliance, pulled Dancer back down to a trot, then a walk. It wouldn't do to guide him over hazardous ground while she was unable to see clearly. Dancer walked on contentedly, seeming happy with the slower gait after his brief run.

A rider appeared, merely a speck in the distance. Still trying to adjust to the sun's intensity, Lizzie found it impossible to tell who it was. Dancer's step never faltered, but Lizzie felt unaccountably nervous. She had never before felt uneasy about riding alone on the Bradley range, but she knew the Double B riders should all be occupied elsewhere.

She glanced around. The grassy plain afforded no hiding place, and she was certain the rider must have already seen her. The only possible place of concealment was a clump of cedars a short distance to the north. She would just have to brazen it out.

Lizzie squared her shoulders, then leaned forward to pat Dancer on the neck. "We'll be okay, won't we, Dancer? You're all loosened up now, and you can run like the wind to get us home safely if you need to."

The rider raised his arm and waved in her direction. Lizzie's stomach tightened into a knot. Determined not to show fear, she timidly raised her hand in return. At that, the rider broke into a lope, heading straight toward her.

Lizzie's knees tightened against Dancer, prepared for flight if necessary. As the other horse drew near, she squinted against the sun's glare, trying to make out the rider's identity.

"Lizzie!" The voice sounded reassuringly familiar, and Lizzie realized with delight that it was Tom. A wave of relief washed over her, and every one of her muscles seemed to go slack. She pulled herself together with an effort, telling herself sternly that this time she would make a better showing with Tom. This time she would behave as an adult, not a clumsy, fumbling child who deserved his amusement.

Tom cantered up, pulling his mount to a sliding stop at Dancer's side. "Well, hello there." He grinned, and sparks of blue fire seemed to shoot out of those amazing eyes.

Lizzie, one hand pressed to her throat, was unable to answer. She scolded herself. Was she never going to act like a mature woman around this man?

"You look a little tired," Tom told her. The words were solicitous, but laughter glinted in his eyes, and Lizzie had the feeling he knew exactly how his presence affected her.

"I'm all right," she said. "I just needed to catch my breath."

"Uh-huh."

Lizzie shot a sidelong glance at him, but his expression was innocent. Too innocent, she thought. She had spent too many years around Willie not to recognize the signs.

Tom swung his horse around to walk beside Dancer. "You heading anywhere in particular?"

Lizzie shook her head. "Just riding. I haven't been over this way in a while."

They rode for several minutes before Tom broke the silence. "Getting a little hot, isn't it?" He pulled out his bandanna and wiped the back of his neck.

Lizzie thought the day was surprisingly pleasant, but then, she'd only been out for a casual ride. She didn't know how quickly Tom had covered the distance between the ranch and here.

"How about taking a rest in those cedars?" he asked suddenly. "I could use some shade, and I wouldn't mind some pretty company to go with it."

Lizzie hesitated, wondering if that was wise. *Grow up,* she told herself impatiently. *You don't want him to think you're a baby, do you?* "All right," she said softly. "Just for a little while."

Tom's horse led the way into the cedar grove. The trees rose thirty feet above them, spreading their limbs to form a sheltering canopy. *It's almost like entering another world,* Lizzie thought. The welcome shade both refreshed and protected them, screening them from the view of anyone outside while allowing them to see out quite clearly.

In silence, Tom helped Lizzie dismount. Accustomed to fending for herself, she was unused to this kind of attention, and the warmth of his hands at her waist threatened to unnerve her completely. She clamped her lower lip between her teeth as he ground-tied the horses, wondering if she had made a grievous mistake.

Tom led Lizzie to a fallen log and seated her upon it with a gallant bow, then took his own seat on the ground nearby. Lizzie fidgeted nervously, twisting her hands together and keeping her eyes fixed on the toes of her boots. What was she thinking of, putting herself in a situation like this?

She did nothing but look like an absolute fool every time she was around Tom, and this time would be no different. She might just as well get on Dancer and —

"Lizzie," Tom spoke softly, his voice caressing her name.

She raised her gaze as far as his top shirt button, unwilling to meet his eyes.

"Lizzie, look up. Look at me," he said.

Slowly, reluctantly, she obeyed. His eyes glowed an even deeper blue than usual. Unable to tear her gaze away, she stared back, her heart beating wildly.

"I'm glad I saw you," he said. "I've been wanting to talk to you alone ever since I met you."

"You — you have?" Lizzie's voice came out in a timid squeak.

His smile made her shiver inside. "Is there something I do that makes you nervous? You seem skittish every time I come around."

Lizzie groped for the right words to say. Yes, he made her nervous. Yes, she totally lost her composure whenever he was near. But she could never admit that to him!

She managed a weak smile. "I'm fine," she said, not altogether truthfully. "I'm glad you came along, too." The words were out of her mouth before she could stop them. She felt appalled by her boldness.

To her relief, Tom seemed to accept her answer and he leaned back, relaxed. "That's good," he said and added, "Are you hungry? I've got some lunch in my saddlebags."

Lizzie nodded. "I could eat something," she admitted. She watched Tom carry his saddlebags to the log and unpack a blanket and several packets of food. Spreading the blanket before her, he set out ample quantities of bread, cheese, and fried chicken. Lizzie looked at the food, realizing it was more than one cowboy, even a hungry one, would bring along just for himself. Her heart beat faster, and she wondered if this meeting might not have been accidental after all.

Tom sat cross-legged at the far edge of the blanket, and after a moment's hesitation, Lizzie slid off the log and sat on the ground facing him. She bit into a drumstick, trying to pretend they were on an outing her parents knew about and approved of.

"Tell me about yourself," she ventured, surprising herself again.

Tom looked pleased at this sign of interest. "There's not a lot to tell," he began. "I was born in east Texas. My pa died of cholera, and my ma ran off with a dry goods drummer when I was twelve. I've been on my own ever since."

Lizzie gaped, trying to imagine what it must have been like. "How awful!" she exclaimed. "How did you manage?"

"I hired out to a neighbor at first, wrangling horses. Then I went to Fort Worth and trailed a herd over to Chisum's ranch. One time or another, I've done a little bit of most everything. I've met a lot of people and seen a lot of country while I was doing it. Now I'm here." His eyes glinted at Lizzie. "And it's a mighty pretty place to be."

Lizzie felt a blush creep up her cheeks and reminded herself not to take his words personally.

"What about you?" Tom asked.

"Me?" She stared at him blankly.

"I know you're the boss's daughter. I know that you go out riding nearly every day and that you've got the prettiest gold hair I ever laid eyes on, but that's all I know. I want to know more." He leaned toward her intently. "Lots more."

Lizzie crumbled some cheese between her fingers and racked her brain for something, anything to say that would begin to equal Tom's colorful life. Her own experiences, which up to now had filled her with such contentment, seemed flat and dull in comparison.

"Well," she began, "I was born in Texas, too, but we came here when I was eight, so I've lived here most of my life. I've spent a lot of time riding and doing things with my brother, but I've never been much of anywhere except for one trip back East when I was a little girl. I guess there isn't much to tell," she concluded wistfully.

Tom regarded her thoughtfully. "I think there's a lot more than you know," he said. "And I intend to find out what it is." His voice, warm and husky, melted her nervousness like the snows in spring.

She realized with a start of surprise that, for the first time, she felt comfortable in his presence. Tom stretched out, propping himself up on one elbow, and Lizzie leaned back against the log, enjoying the companionable silence and watching the canopy of branches overhead sway in the wind.

Why have I been so nervous around him? Right now I feel like I've known him all my life. With a burst of energy accompanying this realization, Lizzie got to her feet and began clearing away their picnic, shaking out the blanket and folding it ready to be packed away. Tom stood, too, and took the blanket from her. Their fingers met, and Lizzie felt the tingling sensation that sometimes came with a lightning storm. Tom opened his mouth as if to speak, but at that moment both Dancer and Tom's horse threw up their heads and whinnied, their ears pointing toward the south.

Tom instantly looked in that direction and stiffened. "Someone's coming," he said in a low voice. "Stay here while I go out to meet 'em. If they don't get too close, they'll never know you're here." He shoved the blanket and food wrappings into his saddlebags, threw them on his horse, and mounted. Gathering the reins, he turned to Lizzie and said, "Thank you. It isn't often I get to spend time in the company of a fascinating woman." He touched his horse with his heels, and Lizzie was left alone.

She watched as he trotted out to meet the newcomer, whom she now recognized as Bert. The two men talked for a moment, then rode off together.

Lizzie watched their retreating figures, pressing her fingertips to her lips and reflecting on the way Tom had kept her presence a secret. The simple, chivalrous gesture touched her deeply.

She looked around the place where they had eaten, committing every detail of their time together to memory. How much had changed in that short time!

When she judged enough time had passed, she went to get Dancer. Holding the reins in her hand, she closed her eyes and whispered, "Father, thank You for hearing my prayer and giving me this sign. Please keep on showing me the way."

Chapter 7

Lizzie stood with her face only inches away from her bedroom mirror, looking intently at the girl who stared back at her. Large gray eyes fringed by dense lashes widened when she realized with a sense of wonder that not an ounce of baby fat remained on the delicate oval face. Her fingertips lightly traced the reflection from the curve of the brow to the small but determined chin.

Stepping back, she could see her fair hair, loosened for the night, cascading past her shoulders like a waterfall. She brushed the golden waves behind her shoulders and looked critically at her camisole-clad figure. When had she developed that trim waistline? And when she looked at her profile, there were curves she hadn't noticed before.

She caught her breath in a ragged gasp. *It's true. I'm not a little girl any longer. I'm a woman — a "fascinating" woman,* she corrected, hearing Tom's remark again in her memory. Flinging her arms wide, she spun around her room, delighting in her discovery.

She changed quickly into her nightdress, blew out the lamp, and slipped between the sheets, hugging the newfound knowledge to her in the darkness.

An hour later, sleep still had not come. Rising, Lizzie pulled on her robe and stole barefoot down the corridor to her special haven, the courtyard in the center of the hollow square formed by the four wings of the house.

She crept across the patio, its flagstones still warm from the day's heat, and picked her way to the enormous cottonwood tree that stood sentry in the courtyard's center. Seating herself on the bench that encircled the trunk, she drew her knees up under her chin and leaned back against the rough bark. She tilted her head upward, gazing in delight at the stars overhead.

There they were — the North Star, the Big Dipper, and other constellations she had known since childhood — beaming down on her like old friends.

And somewhere, she knew, even bigger and brighter than these glowing points of light was the One who had created them all. The same One who had created her and loved her and was even now working out amazing things for good in her life.

"Lord," she breathed, her voice no louder than the whisper of night air that rustled the leaves above her, "it's hard to realize sometimes that in Your whole, vast creation You can look down and find me, but I'm so glad You can. Thank You for loving me and guiding me and bringing me to this point in my life. I'm so happy right now. So *very* happy!"

Lizzie sat like that for some time, the sounds of the night creatures whispering their own songs of praise in harmony with the melody in her heart, before she returned to her bed. This time she slept.

Shrill whinnies pierced the air, punctuated by the staccato beat of nervous hooves on packed earth. Adam hooked one boot heel over the bottom rail of the corral and rested his elbows on the top rail and watched Charles study the select group before him.

Charles eyed first one horse, then another, looking them over with an expressionless face. Finally, he pushed himself away from the corral fence and stared straight at Adam.

"There's a problem," he said bluntly.

Adam felt knots form in his stomach. He straightened slowly, as if waiting for a blow.

"What do you mean?" The horses he had brought up today for Charles's inspection were his finest stock.

Charles looked at him thoughtfully and narrowed his eyes before he spoke. "Yep, a problem. They're all so good, I can't make up my mind which ones to take." He guffawed in delight when Adam finally absorbed the meaning of his words and sagged back against the top rail.

"You had me going, there," Adam admitted. "I'm glad you like 'em."

Charles shook his head in admiration. "It beats me how you can take those sorry-looking broomtails that eat up our range and turn them into good cow ponies. You really have a gift for this, Adam. Once the word spreads, it won't surprise me a bit if you become one of the top horse breeders in the territory."

Adam turned to look at the horses, as much to hide the emotion that gripped him as anything. After all the years of planning, the long, grueling hours of work, this affirmation was sweet indeed. Having the praise come from the man who was not only his employer, but the father of the woman he loved, made it doubly sweet.

He cleared his throat, hoping the rising emotion wouldn't be evident in his voice. "You still haven't said which ones you want."

"Pick out the best three, Adam. I trust your judgment."

The sound of light laughter reached them, and the two turned to see Lizzie and Willie approaching the barn. Willie said something to his sister, and she responded with more laughter.

Charles watched his children with a fond smile, and Adam noted the way the sunlight glinted off Lizzie's hair. She looked even lovelier than usual.

Someday, he promised her silently, *someday soon, I won't just be one of your father's hired hands. I'll have a place that's fit for you, and I'll be able to tell you what's in my heart.*

When the pair drew nearer, Charles waved to them. Laughing, they waved back. Willie grinned at Adam and called out, "Not a bad-looking bunch you brought in."

"Thanks," Adam responded dryly. And then, "Afternoon, Lizzie."

Her gaze passed right by him to a point

over his shoulder; Adam turned to see Tom Mallory emerge from the barn leading Dancer, saddled and ready to go.

Lizzie swept by Adam without a word.

Charles frowned. "What's gotten into her? That was downright rude." He started to go after Lizzie, but Adam laid a restraining hand on his arm.

"Don't worry about it," he said, his lips tightening in frustration. "She just has her mind on other things."

Lizzie accepted Dancer's reins from Tom and mounted her horse, a slow flush suffusing her cheeks at Tom's look of frank admiration. He held the horse's headstall a moment longer than necessary. Moving so Dancer stood between him and the two men by the corral, he whispered, "Are you going to take the same route you did yesterday?"

Lizzie nodded, hardly daring to hope that he might mean what she thought he did.

Tom gave only a smile and a swift wink in response. He bent as if to check Dancer's front hoof, then straightened and patted the gelding on the shoulder. "Looks okay to me," he said. "You should be just fine." He touched two fingers to his hat brim in salute and sauntered off toward the bunkhouse.

Lizzie tried not to let her excitement show as she waved to her father and rode off. Following her path from the day before, she wondered if Tom truly meant to imply that he planned to meet her again. If so, where would it be? And when? How she wished he had made his meaning clear! The trees, she decided. He would make a point of meeting her at the same place as yesterday.

But when? How could she know when to be there?

In the end, she decided to go just where she had gone yesterday. If Tom knew where she'd been and when and wanted to intercept her elsewhere, she should stick as close as possible to yesterday's schedule.

Lizzie fidgeted as she rode, wishing she were already at the trees and hoping she had chosen the correct course of action. What if he were already there, waiting? What if he had gotten tired of waiting and left before she got there? It would be horrid to spend all this time following yesterday's course, only to find she had misunderstood.

She brooded over the possibility as Dancer continued along in his smooth, easy gait. Was it only the day before that she had taken such pleasure in the scene around her, reveling in its beauty? Now she felt only irritation as the scenery passed by far too slowly to suit her.

By the time the cedars came in sight, she was a nervous wreck. She stood in her stirrups, straining to make out every detail, willing herself to spy Tom or his horse.

Only the trees, the scrub brush, and the gently waving grasses marked the landscape. Tom was nowhere to be seen.

Lizzie stifled a sob, fully realizing only now just how much she had longed to meet him again. *What a ninny you are!* she scolded herself. *He was probably only trying to be friendly, and you've made a big thing out of nothing. Serves you right to be disappointed!*

She swiped the back of her gloved hand across her eyes, dashing away angry tears. The day, which had started out with such glorious promise, now seemed cold and dismal, even though the sun shone brightly.

She kicked Dancer into a lope. She was angry, she told herself, nothing more. Angry at Tom for not speaking plainly, angry at the day for holding out such empty promise, and most of all, angry at herself for her naive assumption that Tom could be interested in her.

And that cold, empty feeling inside her was only hunger.

She decided to stop at the trees after all. She would eat some of the biscuits she had brought along and enjoy the cool shade, all on her own. There was no reason to feel the day was wasted, no reason at all.

It wasn't until she was sliding off Dancer's back that she caught sight of Tom's mount, tethered farther back among the trees. Suspended halfway between the saddle and the ground, she dangled in midair, looking anxiously about for Tom.

His breath tickled the skin behind her ear at the same instant she felt his hands circle her waist and lower her to the ground as easily as if she weighed no more than a sack of oats. A warm flush burned its way up her neck to stain her face, and she felt utterly ridiculous. What a sight she must have made, hanging there gaping!

She whirled around the moment her feet touched the ground, determined to regain some of her lost dignity. But with Dancer immediately behind her and Tom still clasping her waist, she suddenly realized there was nowhere to go. Nowhere at all.

She attributed the uncontrollable

pounding of her heart to her surprise at his appearance and to relief at his being there. A relief so overwhelming it frightened her.

Tom slowly, lazily removed his hands from her waist and placed them against Dancer's saddle, on either side of her shoulders. Apart from her father and Willie and an occasional hug from her uncle, Lizzie had never been this close to a man. She found the experience unnerving.

Unnerving and not altogether unpleasant.

Her glance traveled up the front of Tom's shirt, past the bandanna tied at his neck and the cleft in his chin that deepened when his lips curved in an amused smile, to the fiery blue gaze that held her like a rabbit hypnotized by a snake.

"I thought you'd never get here," Tom said, his breath stirring the loose tendrils of hair at her temples.

Lizzie shut her eyes and fought for control. Her knees had turned to jelly and threatened to give way at any moment. "I wasn't sure where you wanted to meet me," she said, hating the way her voice quavered.

Tom straightened, pulling away from her at last. Lizzie couldn't decide whether she felt disappointed or relieved. He gave a low chuckle, as if satisfied.

"I knew you'd be smart enough to figure out what I meant." He placed a finger under her chin, tilting her face up toward him. "Don't feel bad," he said gently. "I've only been here a little while. It just seemed like hours, waiting for you to show up."

He turned and waved toward the log where she sat the day before. "Come over here. I want to make the most of the time we have."

As he walked beside her, Lizzie willed her trembling legs not to betray her. Was this what love did? Did everyone have this uncontrollable, shaky feeling?

Lizzie was touched by Tom's obvious attempts to make the setting attractive. He had swept the dirt smooth with a cedar branch and cleared away the broken limbs and twigs that had littered the ground. *Yesterday must have meant as much to him as it did to me,* she thought happily. *Otherwise, he'd never have taken such pains.* The knowledge gave her a warm inner glow and a newfound confidence.

She accepted the sandwich Tom handed her, enjoying the tingling sensation she felt whenever their fingertips touched.

Look at him, she told herself, thrilled with her new ability to meet and hold his gaze without dropping her own. *Here we are, all alone. He could have taken advantage of me a dozen times already, if he'd had a mind to. But all we're doing is sitting here, eating and talking. What a perfect gentleman!*

Their conversation went along much the same lines as the last time, with each filling in gaps in their personal histories. Finally Tom turned, shielding his eyes with one hand and gauging the height of the sun. "I'm afraid it's time to pack it in for today," he said, turning back to Lizzie. The regret in his eyes mirrored her own.

Swallowing her disappointment, she helped him clean up the area. *Maybe, just maybe, this won't be the last time.*

She waited for Tom to bring Dancer to her and wasn't surprised when he grasped her at the waist again to boost her into the saddle. He paused before lifting her and stared intently into her eyes. Lizzie felt her heart race and knew for certain that this time it was due to pleasure and not surprise.

"Will you meet me here again tomorrow?" he asked.

She nodded, afraid to trust her voice.

"Good." Tom smiled, and the glow she felt rivaled the sun for its warmth. "I don't always know what I'll be doing from one day to the next, so I can't promise to be here every day. But I'll make it as often as I can and try to let you know when I can't. Is that all right with you?"

Lizzie nodded again, too happy to speak.

"Good," he said again, and this time he did lift her onto Dancer's back. "You go first this time." She could see him standing in the same place, watching her as she rode away.

Lizzie marveled at the way the day had improved. Only a short while ago it had seemed so dead and dismal, and now it was positively radiant. And while she'd been willing to settle for biscuits alone under the cedars, instead she had enjoyed another interlude with Tom.

She laughed softly to herself. This had been better than biscuits. Much, *much* better!

Chapter 8

Two weeks later, Lizzie saddled Dancer and turned him toward Judith's house. Tom wouldn't be able to meet her at the cedars today, so she planned to use the time to work on her mother's quilt. Maybe she'd finish it today. It would be nice to have it done and out of the way.

She knew Judith was anxious to finish it before the baby's arrival and realized with a twinge of guilt that it could have been done earlier if only she'd gone to Judith's more often. But she'd been too busy.

Busy with Tom. She shivered with delight, still hardly able to believe he cared. He had shown her, though, shown her time and again.

They met nearly every day at what Lizzie now thought of as "their" place. Sometimes she would find Tom already waiting and seeming as anxious for their time together as she was. Other times she would arrive first and wait with delicious anticipation, hoping against hope his duties hadn't taken him elsewhere.

On the days when he was unable to meet her and hadn't been able to let her know in advance, she spent the time moving from spot to spot, letting each one spark its own memory. Even now, miles from the grove, she could picture it clearly in her mind's eye.

There was the log where they sat most often, with Tom pleasantly close beside her as they talked and dreamed together. Tom gradually told her more about himself, opening up more, once he realized he could trust her not to judge him too harshly for some of his actions.

He had been involved in several gun battles, he confided, and at first she had been shocked and disturbed by the news. But when he explained the circumstances, how each time it had been in defense of himself or someone weaker, she found herself more in love with him than ever.

Over near the tallest cedar was the spot where she had tripped over an exposed root and would have fallen if Tom had not moved quickly and caught her. She closed her eyes a moment, savoring the memory of being supported in his arms. He held her longer than strictly necessary, but not too tightly, and released her before she became uncomfortable.

And there, by the spot where the horses waited . . . Lizzie breathed a sigh of pure wonder when she remembered their last parting. They spent a perfect hour together. Tom's gaze, always intense, burned with a fire that left her breathless. When it was time for her to mount Dancer, he moved to help her as he always did. But this time, instead of taking hold of her waist to boost her to the saddle, he gently grasped her shoulders and lowered his head toward hers.

She caught her breath now in memory, even as she had when it dawned on her that he was about to kiss her. Her eyelids had fluttered closed of their own accord, and she scarcely dared to breathe, not knowing what to expect. When his lips pressed against hers, she felt as though she were rising through the air, spinning in the sky to dance among the clouds, and thought it was the most perfect moment of her life.

She could still feel the warm pressure of his lips and the hard muscles of his shoulders as she shyly wrapped her arms around his neck. For a moment, she wondered uneasily what her parents would say about this but assured herself they would understand when the time came for Tom to talk to them.

And that time would come soon, she knew. Tom hinted at it only moments after that beautiful, perfect kiss. He looked deep into her eyes until Lizzie felt he was examining her very soul. Then he whispered, "Not much longer, Lizzie, my sweet."

Right now, Lizzie thought, life seemed almost too wonderful!

Once again she rode into the yard, handing Dancer's reins to Sam this time. She watched him strut proudly toward the barn with Travis, his towheaded younger brother, following in his wake.

Rose waited for her in the open doorway. "I'm helping Mama clean the house today," she announced importantly. "She'll be with you in just a minute, as soon as she freshens up. She's been lying down." Her voice lowered and she whispered conspiratorially, "She really needs her rest these days, you know."

Lizzie nodded with what she hoped was an appropriate show of understanding and took her place at the quilting frame while Rose, dust rag in hand, went off to her chores. She could tell at a glance that Judith had worked on the quilt alone since she'd been there last and felt another pang of remorse. Judith had enough on her mind right now without having to carry Lizzie's responsibilities as well. Then she remembered their earlier conversation about God working things out for the best in her life. Since Tom was her answer to prayer, surely Judith couldn't argue about her spending time with him.

Lizzie picked up one of the threaded needles and set to work. Back and forth, in and out, the tiny stitches accented the colorful pattern. *How pretty this will look on Mama's bed!*

Lizzie had started on her second needle when Judith entered the room. "Hello, stranger," her aunt greeted her, smiling. Lizzie flinched a little at the mild rebuke.

"Hello, yourself," she replied brightly, determined not to let anything ruin her beautiful day. "Thank you for the extra work you've done." She took a second look at her aunt and frowned. "Are you feeling all right? You look pale."

Judith waved her hand, dismissing Lizzie's concern. "It's just getting close to time, that's all. It'll all be over soon, then I'll really look pale after all those sleepless nights taking care of the baby."

Her words were intended to be soothing,

but they had just the opposite effect on Lizzie. "Just how close is it? Should you be up and around right now?"

This time Judith laughed. "If babies came exactly on schedule, it would make everyone's life easier. Unfortunately, they seem to have a sense of timing all their own, no matter what date we decide they should arrive." She shifted in her chair, sitting even farther away from the quilting frame than she had the last time.

"As to whether or not I should be up and around," she continued, "if I went to bed and stayed there until the baby came, I might wind up lying around for the next month." Judith grinned, watching Lizzie's wide eyes stare at her bulging midsection in disbelief. "Or he might make his appearance today. Either way, I'd rather be up and going about my business until he comes, instead of sitting on pins and needles the whole time."

Lizzie shook her head and went back to her sewing, wondering if she would be able to show the same energy and fortitude when it was her turn to become a mother. Lost in happy speculation about whether her children would have her blond hair and Tom's cleft chin, she didn't catch Judith's next remark.

"What's that?" she asked when she realized her aunt had spoken.

"I just asked if you'd been all right yourself," Judith answered. "I was a little concerned when you didn't come back to work on the quilt for so long, but Jeff said you weren't ill."

The unspoken question hung in the air between them, and Lizzie searched for a way to satisfy her aunt without telling her too much of her cherished secret.

"I've been fine," she said slowly, "just very busy lately." The answer sounded weak even to her, and she glanced up to see Judith's reaction.

To her surprise, Judith looked as uncomfortable as Lizzie felt. "Lizzie," she began, "may I ask you a personal question?"

"I guess," Lizzie answered, flustered.

"Have you been spending time with Tom Mallory?"

The question caught Lizzie completely off guard, and she floundered, trying to find a way to answer truthfully without saying too much. "I've talked to him some around the corrals." That at least was true, if not the whole truth. She decided to take the offensive and ask a question of her own. "Why do you ask?"

Judith rubbed her hand slowly across her

abdomen several times before she spoke. "I'm not sure how to say this, dear, and I don't want to give offense. It's just that Jeff — well, Jeff has some real concerns about him, and we hoped you weren't . . . getting involved with him, that's all."

Lizzie's eyes widened, and Judith fluttered her hand and laughed nervously. "That didn't come out quite the way I meant to say it." She took a deep breath and started again. "Jeff was out the other day and heard some shooting. When he rode over to investigate, he found Tom Mallory practicing a fast draw." Her expression grew sober. "Jeff said he was good. Very good."

Lizzie felt giddy with relief. "Is that all?" she asked lightly. "It sounded like you thought he was a criminal of some kind."

Judith opened and closed her mouth several times. "But Lizzie, honey, law-abiding people don't go around practicing a fast draw. That's for gunfighters and ruffians."

"No, really, it's all right," Lizzie countered. "Tom's told me all about it. He got involved in a gunfight when he was fifteen. Some drunken bullies were tormenting a poor old man, and Tom stepped in to stop them. They pulled their guns and threatened both him and the old man, and Tom managed to wound the leader and scare the rest of them off before they fired a single shot. He did all that when he was only fifteen. Imagine that!

"Since then there have been other times when the same kind of thing happened. Tom says it's like a gift he has. He's just good with a gun. If he hadn't been there, goodness knows what would have happened.

"And as far as practicing goes," she went on, "once someone gets the reputation of being fast on the draw, there will always be others who come along, trying to prove they're faster. He has to practice, just to make sure he keeps his speed up. He does it to protect himself."

Judith, looking unconvinced, bent over her needlework once more. After a moment, Lizzie followed suit. *Doesn't she understand? It's really so simple.*

They stitched in silence for a time, with part of Lizzie's mind focused on the job at hand and part wondering whether she would see Tom again the next day.

Judith broke the silence. "Is he anything special to you, Lizzie?" she asked quietly, her gaze still fixed on her moving needle.

The need to share her news with someone overcame Lizzie's caution, and the words fairly gushed forth from her.

"I think he is," she confided, trying to maintain some degree of calm. She searched her aunt's face but couldn't gauge her reaction.

"He's kind, he's a gentleman, and . . . and he really seems to think I'm special, too," she said softly, remembering his kiss. "I guess you could say he's pretty special." She wondered if the joy that welled up inside her at the opportunity to speak of him showed in her eyes. She felt as if it lit up her whole being.

Judith drew a long, cautious breath before she spoke again. "What about the gunfighting?" she asked. "Doesn't that concern you?"

Lizzie sighed impatiently. "I told you, it's all been to help other people. Kind of like the knights of old in the books we read together when I was a little girl. They had to fight, too, but it was always to help someone else. People looked up to them then; why can't they appreciate Tom now?"

Judith nodded slowly, as if trying to understand. "Has he ever . . . made advances to you?"

"No!" Lizzie responded hotly. "I told you, he's been a perfect gentleman." The kiss, she told herself, didn't count. Tom hadn't forced himself upon her at all. "A gentleman in every way," she said emphatically.

"All right, honey," Judith said gently. "I didn't mean to imply anything else or pry, for that matter. It's just that Jeff and I care so much for you, and we don't want you to be hurt. You've led a pretty sheltered life here all these years, you know."

" 'Sheltered' is right!" Lizzie replied with a vehemence she hadn't known she possessed. "I've hardly been anywhere or done anything, and Tom's done so much!"

"I wouldn't say you haven't gone anywhere," Judith argued. "There have been quite a few trips with your father to Santa Fe, as I recall, where you've met some pretty influential people. And what about your trip back East? You certainly saw a lot then."

"Oh, that." Lizzie waved her hand. "That doesn't count. I was only a child then, Aunt Judith, a little girl! And I'm not a little girl anymore," she said firmly. "When I hear about the places Tom's been — and on his own, not traipsing along holding on to a grown-up's hand — it makes me realize how little I've done with my life." She sighed. "I want to do more, and I don't want to wait much longer to do it."

Judith sat staring at her for a long moment, then pressed her lips together and glanced down at the quilt. "Look at that," she said, fastening her thread and breaking it off. "It's finished!"

"Let's spread it out and look at the whole thing," Lizzie said eagerly, forgetting her restlessness. Together they removed the quilt from the frame and carried it into Judith and Jeff's bedroom, where they spread it lovingly across the bed.

"It's beautiful," Lizzie said with a happy sigh. Then she looked up at her aunt, frowning. "Isn't it?"

Judith laughed as though the earlier tension had never been. "It is indeed. Your mother will love it. Do you want to take it home with you today?"

"If it's all right with you, I'd like to leave it here until Mama's birthday. We've kept it a secret so long, I'd hate for her to find out about it ahead of time by accident."

Judith nodded her agreement, and they folded it carefully and placed it inside Judith's cedar chest.

"Would you like a cup of tea?" Judith offered.

Lizzie shook her head. "I'd better start

for home," she said, eyeing the clouds through the window. "I don't want to get caught in the rain."

Judith walked her to the door and stood sniffing the rain-scented breeze. "I don't think you're leaving a minute too soon," she agreed. "I'm glad we've finished that quilt. Now I can let the baby come with a clear conscience."

Lizzie laughed. "As if you had much choice in the matter!" She started to leave, then turned back and hugged her aunt fondly. "I want you to know you were right." Judith's eyebrows shot up in surprise.

"About what you said about God working out His plan for my life," Lizzie explained. "I read my Bible and prayed, and it's all coming together, just like you said. It's like my own little miracle!" She gave Judith a swift kiss on the cheek and trotted off to the barn to retrieve Dancer, wishing she hadn't seen the troubled look that clouded her aunt's eyes.

Chapter 9

Adam and Jeff leaned over the papers strewn across Jeff's dining table, talking in low voices and making occasional corrections to the sheets full of figures and diagrams. At the end of an hour, Jeff gave a mighty stretch and stood, rubbing the back of his neck. "How about a break?" he suggested. "I'll go see if Judith's got some coffee on the stove."

Adam nodded agreement but continued adding to the sketch on the sheet before him. He kneaded the bridge of his nose between his thumb and forefinger, as if he could rub away his exhaustion.

He was pleased with his plans and even more pleased that Jeff had volunteered to help him work on them. Being able to bounce ideas back and forth gave him confidence in most of his thoughts and had shown him how to shore up the weaknesses in others. He'd be glad when this particular phase of the project was over, though. He was made for physical action, not this paper and pencil business.

He laid down his well-chewed pencil and walked across the room to look out the window, massaging the tight muscles in his neck. Was this all going to be worth it? Would it be everything he anticipated? He surely hoped so. God seemed to be giving him the go-ahead, so all he knew to do was keep on until he sensed a check in his plans.

Turning, he surveyed the room with pleasure. The heavy wood table, flanked by six sturdy chairs, dominated the center of the room. Knickknacks on the equally heavy sideboard and a pair of framed paintings on the wall provided a balance. It wasn't frilly and feminine, but neither was it overwhelmingly masculine. All in all, he saw it as a thoroughly well-designed room.

Jeff built this home for Judith when they were first married, wanting, in spite of his close relationship to his brother and Abby, to keep enough distance between them that his own family could flourish on their own. He had done a good job, Adam thought with approval. It was a home large enough to house a growing family, along with all the love and laughter they could produce. The kind of home he wanted to make for Lizzie . . .

And that's what it all came down to. Adam brushed a wave of hair out of his eyes and scooped up the notes and drawings, arranging them in neat stacks and wishing he could bring similar order to his thoughts.

He had known how he felt about Lizzie Bradley for ages. He'd worked and saved his money like a miser, waiting for the time he could have something good enough to offer her. Until the prospect of owning his own ranch opened up, the likelihood of achieving that goal had seemed like a distant dream.

Now that his long-held goal looked as if it were about to become reality, he had to remind himself that Lizzie needed time to catch up to his desires. Adam was painfully aware that Lizzie considered him a comfortable part of the background — always there but of little personal interest to her. Until recently, though, he thought his chances of catching her interest would be pretty good when the time was right.

Until the intrusion of Tom Mallory, that is.

Now Lizzie was more distant than ever. Distant, dreamy, and to all appearances, utterly captivated by Tom. Adam clenched his teeth together. *Why did he have to show up now? And why here, of all places?*

Jeff appeared in the doorway, holding a fragrant mug of coffee in each hand and balancing a plate on one arm. "I raided the pantry and came up with some of Judith's oatmeal cookies." He maneuvered the plate and mugs onto the table.

Adam took his mug and sipped gratefully, savoring the feel of the scalding liquid coursing its way down his throat. "That wife of yours sure knows how to make coffee."

Jeff nodded smugly. "I trained her well."

"I heard that!" Judith's voice rang out from the kitchen, and Jeff moved to close the door, grinning sheepishly.

Adam enjoyed watching the byplay between these two. It had just the right blend of tenderness and playfulness. Just what he hoped for himself in a relationship with a wife. In a relationship with Lizzie. "You okay?" Jeff looked at Adam over the rim of his coffee mug.

Adam shook himself mentally, aware he had slipped into a daze. *Keep your mind on the business at hand. Time for daydreaming later.*

"I'm fine," he replied. "Just too many

things on my mind, I guess."

"Uh-huh." Jeff shot a shrewd glance at him, then stared into the depths of his mug.

Now, what did that mean? Adam felt unaccountably defensive. He gestured toward the stacks of papers on the table. "I've been concentrating pretty hard on this lately."

"Hmmm." Looking unconvinced, Jeff leaned his elbows on the table and rested his chin on his fists. "Seems to me that this afternoon is the first time I've seen you really concentrate in quite a while."

Adam straightened his papers once more and reached for his pencil, hoping to avoid Jeff's speculative gaze. Jeff hadn't helped build this ranch into a showplace by being unobservant.

When he looked up again, though, Jeff was still staring at him, an amused grin playing around the corners of his mouth. "Is something funny?" Adam demanded.

"I'm just trying to put two and two together and see what I come up with." Jeff leaned back lazily in his chair. "Let's see . . ." He held up an index finger. "You're in a real fever all of a sudden to get this place of yours fixed up and in operation."

"I've been dreaming of this for years.

You know that," Adam protested.

Jeff held up another finger beside the first. "You walk around like you're in some other world and don't see half of what goes on around you."

"Like I said, I've had a lot on my mind, trying to pull all this together." Adam frowned. "You aren't saying I've been slacking off on my work, are you?"

Jeff continued unperturbed, raising his ring finger as he spoke. "When Tom Mallory comes anywhere near you, I can hear your teeth grinding."

Adam flushed and made a conscious effort to relax his jaws. "You've had your own doubts about him. You told me so."

"And last," Jeff concluded, waving four fingers in the air, "you're uncommonly edgy around a certain Lizzie Bradley." Leaning across the table, he fixed his gaze on Adam's. "You tell me if that doesn't add up to four."

Adam spluttered and started to protest but gave it up as wasted effort. *Who am I trying to kid? He's figured it out, anyway.* "Okay, you've got me," he admitted, his shoulders slumping in defeat. "And I might as well level with you; it feels good to finally be able to talk to someone about it."

Jeff threw back his head and let out a delighted whoop. "I knew it!" he yelled. "I knew it!"

Judith's head appeared in the kitchen doorway. "What's all the commotion, Jeff? Is everything all right?"

Jeff, still crowing, seemed about to pour out his discovery, but after a look at Adam's stricken face, he relented. "Everything's fine, honey," he said. "I just came up with the answer to a mathematical problem, that's all. Sorry if I scared you."

His wife gave both men a quizzical look, then shook her head and disappeared behind the swinging door.

Adam eyed Jeff warily. "Are you finished trying to announce this to the world?"

"I guess I did get a little out of hand." Jeff chuckled. "But why all the secrecy, man? This is great news. Have you spoken to Charles yet?"

"I haven't even spoken to Lizzie," Adam confessed. At Jeff's astonished look, he went on, "I wanted to get everything in place first, have a decent home to offer her before I said anything."

"I can understand that. But you're well on your way now. Why not go to her?"

Adam hesitated before answering. "The timing just doesn't seem right."

"It's that Mallory fellow, isn't it?"

"He's part of it." Adam fought down the jealousy that always rose in him at the very thought of the man. "He seems to be around whenever she is, helping her with her horse, offering to clean her tack for her. He knows what he's doing around women, all right. She can't help but be impressed."

"So get out there and do the same thing. Show her you can be impressive, too."

Adam shook his head. "That's just not me, Jeff. I'm not a flashy show horse, just steady and reliable. And I'm not sure that's what she wants."

"It's the steady ones that go the distance. Lizzie knows that."

"But it's the show horses that get noticed. I've been around here so long that, to her, I'm just part of the scenery."

"Hmmm." Jeff stroked his chin as he thought. "You might be right, there. Seems to me that what you have to do is make yourself flash a little bit, just so you get her attention."

Adam shook his head stubbornly. "I won't try to be something I'm not just to get her to notice me. I've put this in God's hands. If it's His will, she'll love me for who I am. If not . . ." His voice trailed off.

"If not, then I'll have to go on, that's all."

Jeff came around the table and clapped the younger man sympathetically on the shoulder. "Then I'll pray with you that God will work it out the way He wants it to. Now, let's get back to work."

Lizzie sat at the supper table with her family. Jeff and the three children joined them, Jeff explaining that Judith had begged off at the last minute.

"She's tired, mostly," he said in response to Abby's anxious query. "Plus, she said food just doesn't sound good right now, and that's no slur on Vera's cooking," he added with a grin. "She hasn't had much appetite at all with this one. I figured I'd give her an evening alone to rest and not have to put up with all of us."

Lizzie watched her cousins eagerly attack Vera's roast beef and potatoes. Their appetites didn't seem to be affected, she thought in amusement. She looked at her own plate ruefully, noting the barely touched food, and picked up a bite with her fork.

The lively conversation faded to a muted buzz as she thought dreamily of Tom and their last meeting. It had been brief — too brief — but once again he held her and touched his lips to hers at parting. What would it be like, she wondered, when the days of secrecy were over and they could meet openly, with her family's consent? That moment couldn't come soon enough to suit her.

She looked up several times during the meal to find Jeff's gaze on her. *What is he looking at?* She raised her napkin to her mouth to wipe away any traces of food that might be lingering there. That didn't seem to be the problem, though, for he continued to stare at her thoughtfully from time to time.

Talk around the table drifted easily from politics to ranch business to local news. During one lull in the conversation, Jeff cleared his throat and began to speak.

"Guess what I spent the afternoon doing?" When no one ventured a guess, he went on. "Adam McKenzie brought over his plans for his horse ranch, and we worked on them for several hours."

"How are things working out for him?" Charles asked with interest.

"He's really coming along. I can't remember when I've seen anyone work so hard to make a dream come true. He's a fine man, Adam is."

"I couldn't agree with you more,"

Charles replied. "He has the drive and the ability to make quite a name for himself. I'm proud to have been able to help him get started."

"Will he be moving onto his own place soon?" Abby asked with a trace of concern. "I'll hate to see him leave anyway, but especially now when we're shorthanded."

"I don't think he has any immediate plans," Jeff answered. "I think he's just getting things together so the place is ready whenever he is.

"Has he talked to you about what he's doing?" Jeff asked, looking directly at Lizzie.

She straightened quickly, startled at the sudden question. "Me? No. I mean, why would he?" She looked around the table in confusion. "Adam's a good worker, I guess, but why would he want my opinion? I mean, he's just *there*."

"Not like some other people, huh?" Willie's teasing eyes glinted at her, and she blushed hotly, hoping the rest of the family wouldn't pick up on his meaning. Willie had already made it clear he'd noticed her interest in Tom and considered it fair game for any amount of teasing.

To her relief, the conversation turned to other matters, and she was no longer the center of attention.

They were savoring the last bites of apple pie when hooves clattered up outside, followed by the sound of heavy boots on the porch and a knock on the door.

"Dan Peterson!" Charles cried with delight when he admitted his longtime friend. "What brings you here? I haven't seen you in a month of Sundays."

"I wish it was something better," replied the weathered rancher, twisting his hat in his hands. "John Pritchard's boy rode down to White Oaks on some business for his pa and stayed over for a dance. A bunch of those wild cowboys who're trying to ape Billy the Kid started raising a ruckus. John's boy took a bullet in the thigh."

Abby's hand flew to her mouth, and Lizzie sank back into her chair.

Charles frowned grimly at the news. "This is bad business, Dan. It doesn't look like things are settling down after all. Man, you must be beat, riding all that way. Come sit down and have something to eat."

Dan shook his head. "I've got to keep moving. It's another couple of hours yet to Pritchard's place. Young Jack will pull through all right, but I need to let his folks know he'll be out of commission for a while. I just thought I'd swing by and tell you the news, Charles. I knew you'd want to know."

Abby hurried from the kitchen with a packet of food, which she pressed into Dan's hands. He thanked her and left, putting an effective end to the light-hearted evening.

"So much for your hero, Willie," Charles said, giving his son a dark look. Willie responded by throwing his napkin on the table and stomping out the door, leaving his parents looking worriedly at each other.

Lizzie excused herself and went to bed early, a jumble of ideas whirling through her head.

Chapter 10

Lizzie's thoughts continued to be muddled over the next few days. Tom went to the south range, sent there by Charles to determine whether enough water remained in the water holes to get them through the summer. Lizzie tried to console herself with the thought that it showed her father's trust in Tom and would prove valuable to them in making their case to her parents when the time came, but such hopeful thoughts did little to ease her mind.

She hadn't realized how much of her time had been spent trying to meet with Tom until he was nowhere nearby. For the first time in her life, she felt absolutely at loose ends. The quilt was finished, and she had no other projects to occupy her time.

Willie found her mooning by the corrals late one morning. "What's the trouble, Sis?" he asked in his old easygoing manner. Lizzie felt encouraged. Willie had grown increasingly sullen and withdrawn over the past few weeks.

"I was trying to decide what to do next, that's all," she said, making the effort to sound cheerful. Willie had been her companion all her life, and she didn't want to lose that closeness.

"Would it perk you up any if I gave you this?" His eyes held their old familiar sparkle as he took a folded piece of paper from his shirt pocket and dangled it before her.

Lizzie's forehead crinkled in confusion. "What is it?" she asked. "Where did you get it?"

"Let's just say that it's a note that's supposed to be handed to you, dear sister. I'm not going to tell you where it came from." He held the paper tantalizingly above her head, moving it just out of reach as she made a grab for it.

"Willie, give that to me!" she cried in exasperation, jumping up to try to snatch the note. "You may be sixteen, but you don't act like you've grown up one bit!"

Willie only grinned at her own childish behavior and flicked his wrist, sending the note spinning through the air and fluttering into Lizzie's outstretched hands. She started to unfold it eagerly, then remembered his curious gaze and creased it shut again. "All right, you've delivered your note. Now get on back to whatever it is you're supposed to be doing." She gave him a little push to start him on his way, and after one last knowing look, he sauntered off, grinning smugly.

Lizzie fumbled at the edges of the note with unaccountably trembling hands and smoothed it open.

Dear Lizzie,

I've missed you and our time together these last few days. It's shown me how important you are to me. I can get away for a little while today. Meet me at our special place at noon. There's something I want to ask you.

Tom

Her hands weren't the only things shaking now. She was trembling all over, like the time she'd had a high fever. It wasn't fever that affected her now, though.

She breathed a happy sigh as she traced her finger across his name and went over the note again, more slowly this time, trying to read the meaning between the lines. He missed her! She savored that delicious thought as she continued reading.

"There's something I want to ask you." What could he mean by that? What could he possibly mean, except . . . She caught her breath, hardly daring to allow herself to believe he might be ready to declare himself this very day. *Settle down. You'll find out soon enough. Just wait until noon.*

Noon? She checked the position of the sun and gasped. She had barely enough time to reach the grove by then if she started right now, and Dancer wasn't even out of his stall yet.

Lizzie raced into the barn, where Willie sat braiding a lariat. He glanced up idly when she rushed past him. "What's chasing you?" he asked.

"Leave me alone, Willie," Lizzie panted. "I need to get Dancer saddled, and I'm in a hurry." She rushed to the end stall, wrenched the door open, and hustled the startled Dancer back down the aisle.

Willie met her, brush and saddle blanket in hand. "Let me help," he offered, performing the grooming and saddling chores with effortless efficiency. Lizzie swallowed her surprise at his offer and used the time to catch her breath and try to regain her composure.

"Thanks, Willie," she said, accepting the reins he held out to her. Swinging into the saddle, she looked down on her brother with a warm surge of affection. "I really appreciate it. You're always there for me when I need you, aren't you?"

Willie just waved and returned to his braiding. Lizzie urged Dancer into a lope and galloped away.

Approaching the grove, Lizzie let out a sigh of relief when she realized Tom was nowhere in sight. She had ridden hard, harder than she preferred to, but it was worth it, as she had apparently beaten him to their meeting place. She was glad she would have a few minutes to calm down. It wouldn't do to meet him looking flushed and anxious.

Lizzie slowed Dancer to a relaxed pace and walked him the rest of the way, taking the time to look around carefully. This was a day she would remember for the rest of her life, and she wanted to commit every last detail of the scene to memory.

Had the sun ever shone more brightly or the scent of the rain-washed cedars smelled sweeter? The wildflowers, having received the life-giving summer rains, stood proud and erect, showing themselves to their best effect. Even the clouds drifted lazily overhead today, not in threatening clusters, but scattered in light patches across the sky. *The day could not be more perfect.* Except for one thing. *I only need Tom here to make it complete.*

Lizzie tethered Dancer and nervously patted at her hair, wishing she had a mirror and comb. On this day of all days, she wanted to look her best.

The sun was now directly overhead. *Straight up noon. He'll be here any minute.* She craned her neck, scanning the horizon in all directions, but no rider appeared.

She paced back and forth within the shelter of the trees, casting an envious look at Dancer, who was contentedly munching on clumps of grama grass. "Look at you," Lizzie told him. "As long as you have food in front of you, you're not worried a bit." She pressed a hand to her own stomach as it rumbled at the mention of food. "See what you've done?" she scolded the horse affectionately. "You've gone and made me hungry. How can I even think about food at a time like this?"

Maybe Dancer had the right idea, Lizzie thought, after another spell of fidgety pacing. She needed something to keep her mind off her nerves and the fact that Tom was overdue. Glancing around for inspiration, her eyes lit on some wildflowers, covered with blooms after the recent rains. Splotches of white, yellow, and purple dotted the ground. They would make a lovely bouquet, she decided, and she began to gather an armful.

Carrying her prize back under the trees, she sat on a smooth, flat rock and began to sort through the flowers, discarding any that were broken or wilted. She wanted to keep only the perfect specimens. When she got home, she could press a sample of each kind of flower as a reminder.

Lizzie looked up again at the sun, measuring its movement across the sky with a practiced eye. She had been there for at least an hour. Where could Tom be? She curled up under a cedar and continued to wait.

In the next hour, Lizzie wove a chain of wild asters, made herself a garland, and stripped all her discarded blooms of petals while reciting, "He loves me, he loves me not." The last petal made it come out "he loves me not," and she flung it away in disgust.

The sun was now a bright ball dropping lower in the sky, and Lizzie was forced to admit that Tom wasn't coming. Angry tears stung her eyes. He had cared enough to send her the note; how could he have changed his mind so quickly? If he lost his nerve, the very least he might have done was ride by and make sure she was all right, instead of keeping her waiting, hungry, and alone.

The tension and anticipation that filled her ever since Willie gave her the note had built up like a summer thunderstorm and needed some release. Lizzie mounted Dancer and started home without a backward glance, trying to keep her pent-up emotions in check. She succeeded until she was almost in sight of the ranch buildings. Then tears of humiliation pricked at her eyes, and she felt their hot sting as they coursed down her cheeks.

Lizzie bit her lip to keep from sobbing aloud. If she could just make it to the barn without meeting anyone! There, alone in its concealing shadows, she could let her tears run freely. No one need know of her disappointment.

No one stirred as she rode closer. Her whole attention was focused on reaching the barn unseen. Only a few more yards now, and still no one appeared. . . .

She had made it. Slipping from the saddle, she gathered the reins in her hand and hurried inside the barn. Dancer nuzzled her shoulder from behind, and she turned to bury her face in his silky mane. Relief at reaching her goal made her weak, and she clung to the horse for strength to remain upright.

"Why?" she whispered in an agony of spirit, as though the horse could understand and answer. "Why did he send that note and then not come?" Sobs rose in her throat, and with no reason now to hide them, she let them come, great racking sobs that shook her whole body.

The scrape of a boot sole against gravel warned her she was not alone. Swiftly she dashed the tears from her face with the back of her hand and busied herself undoing the cinch strap.

"Hi, Sis." Willie lounged against the partition behind her. "Just getting back?"

Lizzie flickered a quick glance his way, then turned back to her work, determinedly keeping her face from him. "Mm-hm." Her voice came out as a tiny squeak, and she had to clear her throat and try again. "Yes," she said flatly. "I'm just now getting home." She slid the saddle from Dancer's back and began brushing his coat vigorously.

"Where were you heading in such an all-fired hurry anyway?" Willie continued to lean against the wall as if he didn't have a care in the world, but Lizzie could detect a speculative gleam in his eye.

"I–I had to meet someone." Lizzie hoped her voice was steady enough to fool her brother. She placed her hand on Dancer's rump and circled to his off-side, working to remove the crust of sweat.

Her concentration was broken by a rasping sound, and she swung around to see Willie, lips pressed together, trying to stifle a laugh. When he saw her puzzled expression, he threw his head back and burst into a loud guffaw.

"You believed it!" he cried delightedly. "You swallowed the whole thing, hook, line, and sinker!"

Lizzie felt the blood drain from her face, and she stared at Willie, now convulsed in laughter.

"What do you mean, I 'believed it'?" she asked slowly, unwilling to accept the dreadful idea taking root in her mind.

"The note!" Willie chortled. "I thought you'd see right through it, but there you went, tearing out of here like a nest of hornets was after you. I bet you've been out there waiting for him to show up all this time, too, haven't you? Whew, I thought you'd fallen for him, but you've got it even worse than I thought!"

Lizzie tried to speak, but her numbed brain couldn't seem to form any words.

"Do you . . . do you mean the note didn't come from Tom after all?"

"You should have seen your face when I gave it to you," Willie gasped, so engrossed in his mirth that he didn't see the murderous look Lizzie turned on him. "I thought you'd figure it out in the first minute or two, but no, you went ripping out of here, then you spent half the afternoon sitting out there waiting for him. That's got to be the best joke I ever — oof!" He grunted when Lizzie launched herself straight at him.

Lizzie, unable to think clearly at this point, knew only that her anger must have some object, and the only object at hand was Willie. She flailed at him with both fists, something she hadn't done since they were children.

Caught off-guard and off-balance, Willie was unprepared for the whirlwind onslaught. He threw up his hands, trying to protect himself from the blows, but the force of Lizzie's attack threw him backward and he landed in the corner in a heap.

"All right, Sis. Enough!" He caught at

her wrists, but Lizzie, empowered by un-reasoning rage, had the upper hand. One wild swing caught Willie on his nose, which spurted a crimson stream of blood.

"Ouch, Lizzie! Cut it out; this is getting out of hand." Willie scrambled to his knees but couldn't regain his feet, and the blows continued to rain down on him unabated.

"Stop it, Lizzie! I'm serious, now." Willie sounded concerned. "Come on, you've always been a good sport. Where's your sense of humor?"

Lizzie, blinded by tears, was deaf to his pleas. She was focused on only one thing — to hurt Willie as much as he had hurt her — and to that end she was giving her all.

Her attack was interrupted when a pair of muscular hands encircled her waist, lifted her off of Willie, and set her firmly on the ground. Her arms pummeled the air for a few moments before she realized she no longer had a target. She covered her face with her hands and heaved in great gulps of air.

"What's going on here?" asked a bewildered voice, and she looked up to see Adam McKenzie's worried face looming over her.

Lizzie risked a look at Willie, just getting

to his feet. Streaks of blood smeared his face and shirt, and a large welt was beginning to rise on one cheekbone. If his betrayal hadn't left such a raw wound, she might have felt sorry for him.

Willie glared at her in return, wiping his nose with one arm and adding another streak of blood to his shirt sleeve. "What's the matter with you, anyway?" he demanded. "It was just a joke."

"Just . . . a joke." The words were forced out through clenched teeth. Lizzie had no desire to do anything but be alone with her own misery. She turned and stumbled toward the house, oblivious to Adam's voice calling her name.

She reached her room without meeting anyone else and flung herself face down across her bed, wishing the floor would open up and swallow her whole.

Adam stared out the barn doorway, wondering what exactly had happened. Just after Lizzie stormed out, Willie left, shrugging off Adam's restraining hand as well as his questions. Willie then mounted his horse, which had been tied to the corral, and rode off north.

Adam felt as though he had been caught in a hurricane. He tried to give himself time to calm down and think clearly by putting the barn back into some kind of order. He finished grooming Dancer and put the uncharacteristically nervous horse into his stall, giving him an extra measure of grain as a consolation.

The extra time did not help clarify the situation. He had seen those two get into scraps before, but this . . .

He shook his head, glancing in turn from the house to the direction Willie had taken. This was like nothing he had ever seen before and completely out of character for both of them.

Something needed to be done, that was obvious, and no one else had witnessed the scene. It looked like he was the one to get to the bottom of things. He looked once again toward the house. He could hardly go barging in there, demanding admittance to Lizzie's bedroom. He nodded, his mind made up. It would have to be Willie who gave him the answers.

Lord, I could sure use a good dose of wisdom about now. He headed off to saddle his horse.

Nearly an hour later, he was still on Willie's trail. *The boy must have ridden like the wind. He knows better than to —* Adam drew his mount up sharply at the sound of rapid gunshots.

The shots had come from just beyond a nearby rise. Adam swung out of the saddle and ran uphill, crouching low as he neared the top.

Cautiously he peered over the crest. Willie stood below him, gun in hand, and Adam, with a hand on the butt of his own pistol, looked around wildly to locate the attacker.

Willie, however, seemed unconcerned. He thumbed another round of cartridges into the cylinder and replaced the gun in its holster. Spreading his feet to shoulder width, he crouched into a gunfighter's stance.

Suddenly his hand whipped the pistol from the holster and raised it, aiming at a row of bottles set up fifteen yards away. The gun bucked in Willie's hand, and Adam counted five more shots in quick succession. No bottles were left standing.

The worry, tension, and utter confusion that had built up inside Adam whirled into an explosion of anger. Springing to his feet, he descended the hill with giant strides and grabbed Willie roughly by one arm, swinging the boy around to face him.

"What in the world do you think you're doing?" Adam bellowed.

Willie's whole being registered panic at first. Recognizing Adam, he relaxed into an attitude of proud defiance.

"Not bad, huh?" he asked, nodding toward the scattered shards of glass.

Adam let go of Willie's arm and raked his fingers through his hair in exasperation, knocking his hat to the ground in the process. "Have you and your sister both gone crazy?" he demanded.

Willie moved away, swaggering slightly. "Tom's been teaching me." He refilled the empty cylinder. "I think I've got the hang of it."

"Tom," Adam repeated. "And just why does Tom think you might need to know how to do this?"

Willie shrugged. "A man's gotta know how to protect himself. If I ever get in a tight spot, I'll know what to do."

Adam's eyes flashed. "One of the easiest ways to protect yourself from trouble is not to get into tight situations in the first place. Or didn't Tom mention that?" He picked up his hat, slapped it against his leg to knock off the dust, and turned to leave.

"You don't like him, do you?"

Adam turned back to see Willie eyeing him belligerently. He took a slow, deep breath. "No," he said truthfully, "I guess I don't."

"I thought so," Willie said, with some satisfaction. Adam turned again to leave, and once more Willie's words stopped him. "Lizzie does, though."

Adam wanted to walk away as quickly as he could, but his feet brought him to an unwilling halt of their own accord. The truth he longed to avoid was being driven home to him with hammerlike blows. He turned back to Willie. "I guess I knew that," he said evenly. "What was wrong with her today, anyway?"

"Oh, that." Willie snorted. "She can't take a joke, that's all. I gave her a note from Tom, asking her to meet him. Only it wasn't from Tom; I wrote it myself. I thought sure she'd catch on, but she rode out as soon as she'd read it. She spent a good bit of time out there, too, waiting for him to show up." He chuckled in remembrance. "Then when she got back and found out I'd set her up, she jumped me like a wildcat." His fingers touched the welt on his cheekbone. "I don't know what the problem was. It was just a little joke."

Adam held himself firmly in check, not following the impulse to close the distance between them and throttle Willie. Only his hands, clenching and un-clenching at his sides, betrayed his thoughts. He turned without another word and strode away.

Chapter 11

Adam's thoughts whirled on his way back. "Has the whole world gone crazy?" he muttered to himself. Willie, whom he had always looked on as a younger brother, was sure acting like it, with his cocky new attitude and his admiration for Tom.

Lizzie, too, had been acting like a madwoman when he pulled her off her brother earlier. He shook his head ruefully, remembering how he had hesitated to take hold of her, not knowing if she would turn on him next. Yes, Lizzie was acting unbalanced, and the cause for that, too, was tied to Tom Mallory.

And what about himself? Adam snorted derisively. *He* was definitely crazy. Crazy to get involved in Willie's and Lizzie's brawl, crazy to try to straighten out a kid who obviously didn't want straightening out, and crazy — definitely, absolutely, certifiably crazy — to have fallen in love with a woman who was smitten with someone else.

Lord, what's going on? Things have always been so peaceful and straightforward around here, but lately it seems like everything's turned upside down. Show me the way so I can know what You want me to do.

Topping a low hill, he spotted Tom Mallory, back from the south range and riding in to headquarters. Adam spurred his horse into a lope and set his course to intercept Tom's.

Tom seemed surprised to see Adam bearing down on him and pulled his horse to a stop. He tilted his hat farther back on his head and met Adam with an inquiring grin.

Adam reined in beside Tom and spoke abruptly. "You've been teaching Willie to fast draw."

Tom's grin widened, and he leaned back lazily in his saddle. "The boy wanted to learn," he said. "No harm in it."

"Don't you think you should have checked with his father first?"

Tom chuckled. "He's almost a man. When I was his age, I'd been taking care of myself for years. He's got to grow up sometime, and if his daddy won't let him, he'll find a way to do it on his own." He tipped his hat mockingly and rode away.

Adam watched him through slitted eyes. This was beyond anything he could handle alone. He needed help, and he needed it now.

"I've been afraid something like this would happen." Jeff hooked a boot heel on his porch railing and looked at Adam with troubled eyes. "I've seen Mallory shooting." He shook his head. "This is a bad business, Adam."

The younger man nodded his agreement. "I guess I'm a coward. By rights, I should have gone straight to Charles, but I didn't know how to tell him. I was almost hoping you'd tell me I was overreacting."

"I wish I could." Jeff straightened reluctantly. "Let's go get it over with," he said. "We'll tell Charles together."

Adam wished he could be anywhere else when Jeff tapped on the door of his brother's study. When Charles called for them to enter, he wished it even more. Instead of its usually amiable expression, the older brother's face wore an exhausted frown.

"What is it, Jeff?" His weary tone matched his countenance. The man looked like he carried the weight of the world on his shoulders already, Adam thought. And they were about to add to his concerns.

"Nothing good, I'm afraid." Jeff waved Adam to a seat and closed the door behind them. "I'll get right to it, Charles. How much do you know about Tom Mallory?"

Charles's eyes narrowed. "Only what I saw the day I offered him a job and what I've seen since, which is that he seems to be a hard worker who knows what he's doing and does it well. Why?"

"Have you noticed the way Willie's been following him around?"

Charles threw his hands in the air and shook his head. "What that boy is thinking lately is anybody's guess. It's sure beyond anything *I* can understand. He needs someone to look up to, and if Tom Mallory can be a good influence, I suppose I can't complain."

"Even if he's teaching your son to be a gunfighter?"

Utter quiet blanketed the room. Charles froze, his gaze darting between Jeff and Adam. "What are you talking about?" he demanded.

"I've seen Mallory out in the hills, practicing. He's good, Charles, and fast — really fast. And Adam here had an encounter with Willie today. Tell him what you saw, Adam."

I'd just as soon be roping rattlesnakes as this. Adam recounted the scene. He watched Charles's eyes take on a stony glint and his lips tighten into a thin, hard line. Charles started to rise, looking like a man ready to take decisive action.

"Simmer down." Jeff spoke quietly but firmly. "There's more." Charles gaped at him and slid back into his chair with a thud.

"Lizzie came over to visit Judith the other day," Jeff continued. "It seems the subject of one Tom Mallory came up, and Lizzie went on and on about him. I've talked to Judith about my concerns, and she tried to help Lizzie see what kind of person he is, but no luck. Lizzie has stars in her eyes where the fellow's concerned."

Charles groaned and buried his face in his hands. "I've been worried sick about the political situation. Looks like I should have been worrying about things closer to home instead."

He slammed a fist on his desk, sending a bottle of ink skittering perilously close to the edge. "What's he trying to do, corrupt my whole family?" He rubbed a weary hand across his face, the picture of dejection. "If we weren't so short-handed, with Hank laid up, I'd fire him on the spot. As it is, I'll have to keep him on until after roundup. But you can count on me putting him on notice. There will be no contact — *none* — between him and any member of the family except Jeff and me. And woe unto him if he tries to defy me!"

The door swung open just wide enough to admit Lizzie's head. "Oh," she said dully when she saw the three men talking. "I didn't mean to disturb you. I'll come back later."

"Stop right there," Charles commanded. "I need to talk to you, and now's as good a time as any. No," he said when Adam and Jeff moved to leave. "You both know what's going on. You might as well stay."

Those rattlesnakes are looking better and better, Adam thought. Lizzie entered the room hesitantly. Adam studied her face closely, seeking a clue to her present condition.

Traces of the emotional storm still lingered. Her eyes were puffy, and red blotches stood out against her pale skin, hinting at the earlier tears. A faint bruise was beginning to show along the knuckles of her right hand. Adam figured that must have been where she'd connected with Willie's cheekbone.

Lizzie stopped just inside the room and

pressed her back against the wall. Her look flitted from Charles to Jeff to Adam and back to Charles, reminding Adam of a trapped bird facing a group of hungry cats.

"I just came in to borrow a book," she said uneasily. "I can wait."

"What I have to say can't wait." Charles fixed his daughter with a long, measuring look. "Sit down," he ordered without further preamble.

Moving mechanically, Lizzie slid into the leather chair facing Charles's desk. She sat warily, shoulders tensed and hands clasped tightly in her lap, making the resemblance to a trapped creature even more pronounced. She hunched her shoulders slightly and lowered her head, as if awaiting a blow.

Adam's heart went out to her. If he could, he'd sweep her up in his arms and carry her out of there, regardless of her father's presence. But he didn't have that right, he reminded himself bitterly.

"What's this I hear about you and Tom Mallory?" Charles demanded. Lizzie flinched as if a blow had indeed been struck.

Her face ashen, she raised her chin and met her father's angry gaze. "I don't know what to tell you until I know what you've heard," she said with a touch of defiance.

Charles let out a deep breath that was almost a growl. "It has come to my attention," he said, measuring his words, "that you're sweet on Mallory. It has also come to my attention that this swain of yours is no better than a common gunfighter, and he's teaching your brother to follow in his footsteps."

"That's not true!" Lizzie leaped to her feet and faced her father across his desk.

"You don't care for Mallory, then?" Charles asked, eyeing her steadily.

"No! I mean . . . I mean . . ." Her voice trailed off as a hot red wave swept up her neck and suffused her face.

Adam could feel her humiliation at having her feelings laid bare in front of the three of them. *Oh, my sweet Lizzie, I hate to see you suffer like this. But you're too good to throw yourself away on someone like Mallory!*

"I think we can see what you mean," her father said grimly. "Just how far has this infatuation gone, Lizzie? Hasn't it occurred to you that a man like that is only interested in —"

"How can you say that?" Lizzie cried. "You don't know anything about him or what he's really like. How can you sit in judgment like this without any proof?"

Charles, making an obvious effort to control himself, steepled his fingers and waited a moment before he spoke again. "It seems to me," he began, "that an honorable man, the kind of man I'd consider as a son-in-law, would come to me openly, instead of sneaking around behind my back and encouraging you to do the same. Just how much more proof do I need?

"And that's just the part that has to do with you," he went on. "I have it on good authority he's been teaching your brother the art of gunfighting. Is this really the kind of man you expect me to approve of?"

"Don't talk to me about Willie," Lizzie put in. "If he's the one who's been filling your head with these wild stories, I wouldn't believe them for a minute. Willie's word isn't always to be trusted."

Her self-control was dangerously close to slipping away completely, Adam thought. He watched the scene uncomfortably, wondering if he'd witness a repeat of the previous explosion. *I'd just as soon not, Lord. One rescue a day is about all a man can deal with.*

"Let's get back to the main issue," Charles said. "In this case, you and Mallory. I don't understand, Lizzie," he said, his voice betraying his hurt. "If you honestly felt something for him, why didn't you talk to your mother or me? Why slip around like this?"

Lizzie drew herself up with what dignity she had left. "It's true. I care for Tom, and he cares for me. We planned to tell you soon. As for why we didn't say anything earlier, just look at the way you're behaving now." Her voice warmed with passion. "Look at the way you've already judged Tom, without ever talking to him yourself. Can you honestly say that if he — one of your employees — came to you and said he wanted to come calling on me, you'd welcome him with open arms?"

It was Charles's turn to look uncomfortable, and Lizzie pressed her advantage. "Can you?" she repeated.

"I don't know, Lizzie," he admitted. "Perhaps not. But that doesn't make your own underhanded behavior any more acceptable."

"My behavior has been just fine all along," Lizzie stormed. "So has Tom's." She strode to the door and yanked it open, pausing to turn back for a parting shot. "You go ahead and believe all the lies you want to. I know Tom's a fine man — and you'll find out the truth someday!" The crash of the door reverberated through the room.

Charles slumped in his chair and let out a long sigh. "I sure put her in her place, didn't I?" he asked ruefully.

Adam excused himself and walked back toward the bunkhouse, deep in thought. That Tom Mallory was wrong for Lizzie was certain. That Lizzie fancied herself in love with him was equally certain. Adam heard her admit her feelings for Tom with increasing despair, each word hitting him like a hammer blow.

He had halfway expected it, although hearing it stated in such unvarnished terms wounded him more than he'd anticipated. What he hadn't been prepared for was Charles's admission that he might not approve a mere ranch hand as a suitor for Lizzie.

Adam tried to console himself with Charles's wholehearted enthusiasm for his ranch. Owning his own spread would mean he would no longer be a hired hand, but a solid businessman.

At least that was how Adam looked at it. But would Charles see it the same way?

Chapter 12

"Rider comin'," Bert announced.

Adam looked up from pounding a new rim into place on a wagon wheel and shaded his eyes with one hand. The sun hovered nearly straight overhead; its brilliant light dazzled his eyes. "Can you tell who it is?" he asked.

"No one I know, far as I can tell," Bert replied.

The rider on the tall chestnut gelding drew up fifteen yards from them. "Mornin'," he drawled, dismounting in one fluid motion. "Or is it afternoon?" An engaging grin turned up the corners of his mouth and brightened his face.

Adam removed his hat and wiped his forehead with his sleeve. "Whichever it is, it's time to break for lunch," he said, returning the stranger's grin. He thrust forth a hand. "Name's Adam McKenzie."

The other man gripped his hand firmly. "Henry Antrim."

"Are you looking for work or just passing through?"

Henry mopped the back of his neck with a bandanna. "Actually, I'm looking for a friend of mine. I was told he was working here. Tom Mallory — you know him?"

Adam narrowed his eyes and examined Antrim more closely. He didn't seem like a bad sort, but Tom Mallory was definitely a wild one. Any friend of his might bear watching.

"Mallory's out doctoring cattle," he said cautiously. "He's not due in until evening."

A voice hailed Adam and Bert from the direction of the ranch house, and they turned to see Willie waving to them from the porch.

"Jeff needs to talk to you both about something," he told them when they met him halfway to the house. "He'd like you to have lunch with us, if you're ready to eat."

Bert grinned. Vera's cooking put their usual bunkhouse fare in the shade. "That won't take much persuadin'," he said. He hesitated and glanced back over his shoulder. "Fellow out there just rode in looking for Mallory," he told Willie. "Maybe we should feed him at the bunkhouse and come see Jeff after lunch."

Adam winced inwardly. Knowing how Willie idolized Tom, he feared the boy would immediately claim any friend of his hero's for his own. He wasn't disappointed. Willie's face lit up as soon as he heard Tom's name, and he went at once to ask Henry Antrim to have lunch with the family. They were too far away to hear Antrim's response, but Adam could see him shake his head and shuffle his feet, seemingly reluctant to accept the invitation.

Adam watched Willie turn on all his persuasive powers, waving his hands for emphasis. Finally, Antrim laughed, clapped Willie on the shoulder, and accompanied him to the house. "I sure hope this is okay," he said quietly to Adam while they washed up on the back porch. "I don't want to push my way into a family meal." Adam reluctantly chalked up one point in Antrim's favor. Tom Mallory, with his overly confident ways, would never have considered turning down an opportunity to have himself included in the family circle.

Jeff, Abby, and Lizzie stood waiting in the dining room when they entered. Vera placed the last steaming serving bowls in place and chuckled when Adam and Bert inhaled the aroma gratefully.

Adam cast a quizzical glance at Charles's empty chair. Abby hastened to explain. "Charles planned to be here, too, but Matt Chambers is talking about selling off his place, and Charles had to go meet with him at the last minute. We were already looking forward to the idea of having you and Bert for dinner, though, so Jeff agreed to play host. The addition of Mr. Antrim is a welcome surprise."

"Thank you, ma'am," the newcomer responded politely. He still seemed somewhat ill at ease, Adam thought, but his reserve appeared to be melting away at the sight of Vera's cooking.

Watching Jeff help Abby into her chair, Adam realized Willie had not made a move to help Lizzie, and he moved toward her. But he had hesitated too long, and Jeff performed that task, as well. Adam berated himself. Here he'd had a perfectly good opportunity to catch her attention while Tom Mallory was nowhere nearby, and he had muffed it.

On second thought, he wondered if Lizzie had any idea who held her chair for her. She sat silent, her eyes fastened on her plate, not seeming to know or care who else was in the room.

Jeff led the family in saying grace, then waited until the platters of food had been passed around to begin talking to Adam and Bert about his idea for fencing a portion of the range.

Following a spirited discussion of the pros and cons, Abby glanced around the table and asked, "Is anyone ready for seconds?" She laughed gently at Bert's haste in taking advantage of the opportunity. "What brings you to the Double B, Mr. Antrim?" she asked, turning to her unexpected guest.

Henry Antrim wiped his mouth with his napkin and took a swallow of water from his tumbler before replying. "I was just passing through, ma'am, and thought I'd look up a friend who works here."

"How nice!" Abby said brightly, looking at the other two ranch hands. "Was it Adam or Bert you came to see?"

"Actually, ma'am," he replied, looking embarrassed once more, "it wasn't either one of them. Tom Mallory's the friend I'm looking for."

Lizzie's head snapped up, her face brightening for the first time since they entered the room.

"You know Tom?" she asked eagerly.

"I should smile I do," Antrim answered,

giving her a thoughtful look. "Known him for years. We've been through a lot together."

Lizzie's face grew even brighter, and Adam laid his fork down on the table. Vera's famous apple pie, so tempting only moments earlier, suddenly lost its appeal.

"Tell us about him," Lizzie requested.

"He's a good man," said Henry Antrim. He forked up a generous bite of the flaky pastry and chewed thoughtfully. "I'm not sure what all you want to hear, but I can tell you he's helped me out of more than one tight spot, and he's as loyal a friend as I've had."

Lizzie lifted her chin and cast a challenging look at both Jeff and Adam. It was obvious to Adam that she was gathering ammunition to use in a future round with her father.

"That's so nice to hear," she answered sweetly.

Henry Antrim shifted in his chair as if sensing there was more to this conversation than appeared on the surface. He scooted his chair away from the table.

"Ma'am," he said, nodding to Abby, "I've enjoyed this meal more than anything I've had in a long while, but I don't want to impose on you any longer. If you'll excuse me, I'll mosey on now and see if I can't run across Mallory on my way."

Abby returned his smile. "It's been a pleasure to have you, Mr. Antrim. I'm only sorry my husband wasn't here to meet you. Feel free to stop in again any time you're passing this way." She rose to escort him to the door, and the rest of the company followed them out onto the porch.

Adam had to admit Antrim wasn't so bad. *If I didn't know he and Mallory were friends, I'd be tempted to partner with him myself. He is one likable fellow.*

Adam stretched, trying to make himself believe he hadn't overeaten. Vera's cooking was way too good to pass up, and he'd done his share to keep it from going to waste. He leaned against the porch railing while the women and Willie returned to the house and watched idly while Henry Antrim checked his cinch and mounted his horse.

Jeff, looking similarly stuffed, watched, too. Beyond Antrim's horse, they saw Charles emerge from the barn. He looked up curiously at Antrim, who touched his hat brim in a casual salute and rode off.

"I wonder when Charles slipped in?" Jeff said idly. "He sure missed a good meal."

"You aren't getting enough home cooking these days?" Adam joked.

Charles stared curiously after the departing guest and walked slowly to join them. "Who was that?" he asked when he reached the porch. "He looked familiar, but I can't place him."

Jeff's mouth quirked up in a half-smile. "An unexpected dinner guest," he answered. "He also happens to be a friend of Tom Mallory's."

Charles halted in midstride. "He ate at my table?"

Jeff nodded in wry amusement. "He showed up at mealtime, and Willie wouldn't take no for an answer."

Charles compressed his lips and shook his head. His eyes followed the horse and rider, growing smaller in the distance. "What was his name?"

"Antrim," Adam answered. "Henry Antrim." Charles swung around to gaze at him in disbelief, then pivoted to stare after Antrim's retreating figure.

Jeff looked as startled as Adam felt. "Something wrong, Charles?" he asked his brother.

Charles looked from Jeff to Adam and back again. His lips were drawn in a thin line, and the skin around his eyes was taut. "I thought his face looked familiar," he stated in a harsh voice. "Henry Antrim also goes by the name Billy Antrim. Also by William Bonney. But he's best known as Billy the Kid."

Jeff and Adam watched in silence as he stormed off, calling for Abby.

Lizzie slipped into her riding skirt with a sense of elation. The unexpected arrival of Henry Antrim at lunch and his championship of Tom buoyed her sagging spirits for the first time in days. The altercation with Willie had been bad enough; the rift between herself and her father was worse. Being dressed down by him in front of Uncle Jeff and Adam had been one of the most humiliating experiences of her life.

Now, though, she had her own ammunition. Mr. Antrim had endorsed Tom's character in no uncertain terms and in front of witnesses, no less! When her father heard about that, he would have to withdraw his objections and give Tom his approval.

He wouldn't like it, she knew, but he was a fair man and would do the right thing. She adjusted her skirt with a smug grin, thinking of how Uncle Jeff and Adam had been present for both scenes and would have to lend support to her story.

Thank You, Lord. You really are making my way plain. She was amazed at how easy it had been to find answers since she'd started asking God for guidance. It was just like she'd heard in sermons all her life. Why had it taken her this long to put it into practice for herself?

The pounding on her door put an abrupt end to her reflections. "Lizzie?" her father bellowed. "Are you in there?"

Lingering resentment from their earlier blowup flared for a moment, and Lizzie wondered nervously what he wanted. Then she remembered her newfound strategy and strode confidently to open her door.

"Come to my office," her father ordered brusquely. "I need to talk to you."

Lizzie followed him along the hallway, hating the feeling that she was a little girl again, about to get a lecture. She was a woman, she reminded herself, and prepared to conduct herself accordingly.

The sight of her mother seated in front of the heavy desk gave her a moment's pause. Abby's face showed signs of strain, and her hands were clasped tightly in her lap. Lizzie wondered if this was indeed about Tom or if something awful had happened. Not Willie! A surge of fear clutched at her heart. Infuriating as he was, she didn't know what she'd do if something terrible happened to her brother.

She had intended to remain standing, even after her father jabbed a finger toward one of the heavy wooden chairs, but her mother's presence and her concern for Willie weakened her resolve, and she found herself sinking obediently into the seat.

"Young lady —" Charles began, halting as Abby raised a hand in protest.

"Not that way, Charles, please," she said. She turned to Lizzie and searched her face carefully. "You remember Mr. Antrim, of course."

The perfect opening! Lizzie sat up straighter and tilted her chin, looking past her mother into her father's stormy eyes. "Of course! Did you tell Papa what he said about Tom?"

"I started to," her mother replied. "But it turned out he had something to tell me, instead. You see, dear, Mr. Antrim isn't quite the man he appeared to be."

Lizzie looked from one parent to the other in confusion. "What do you mean? Are you saying he isn't a friend of Tom's?"

"Oh, I have no doubt he's a friend of Mallory's," Charles said, rejoining the conversation. "That's just the problem."

Lizzie glanced at her mother for illumination. Abby cleared her throat and gave her daughter a sympathetic look. "It appears we've just broken bread with none other than Billy the Kid."

Lizzie sat a moment in stunned silence before she found her voice. "He — Mr. Antrim, I mean —"

"Is the same outlaw who's been causing nothing but trouble throughout the territory."

"I don't believe it!" Lizzie cried hotly.

"Here." Her mother spread a large sheet of paper on the desk. "Your father has a copy of a wanted poster. Look at the picture."

Lizzie looked closely, hoping against hope it was only a superficial resemblance. But even she couldn't deny that the face on the poster was that of their recent guest.

"Even so," she protested, rallying, "it doesn't change all the fine things he said about Tom. It's Tom's character we're concerned with, not —"

"Exactly," her father interrupted. "If he's a close friend of a notorious outlaw, what does that say about his character?"

"Mother, will you make him listen to reason?"

Abby's usually calm voice quavered as she spoke. "I'm afraid I agree completely,

Lizzie. If this is the kind of companion Mr. Mallory chooses —"

Lizzie wheeled and dashed out of the office. Nearly knocking Willie over when they collided in the front doorway, she ignored his startled yelp and headed straight for the barn. She saddled Dancer in record time and rode off like the wind.

Tears blinded her, and she dashed them away angrily. Conflicting thoughts whirled through her mind. Henry Antrim couldn't be Billy the Kid! She rejected the thought, remembering his polite behavior at dinner. But there was no doubt in her mind the picture on the poster was his. Maybe Willie was right in his assessment of Billy. No, she had heard too many stories to believe that, even for a moment. Maybe Tom didn't know what his friend really was. But she had to dismiss that notion, too. They couldn't have been friends for such a long time without Tom knowing all about him.

God, where are You? her soul cried. *I thought You were on my side!*

Lizzie galloped into Judith's yard without bothering to cool Dancer down and tossed the reins to a startled Sammy. "Watch him for me, Sam. I need to talk to your mother."

She burst into the front room without

waiting for a response to her knock and found Judith rising heavily from the settee.

"Lizzie, are you all right?" Concern colored her aunt's voice. "Has something happened at home?"

"It's horrible, Aunt Judith! It's so unfair!" She began to sob out her painful story. Judith sank back onto the couch, her eyes never leaving Lizzie's face throughout her recital. When Lizzie finished, Judith sat still, watching her carefully.

"What can I do?" Lizzie wailed. "I have to make them see they're wrong."

Judith's eyes closed briefly, as if offering up a prayer for guidance. "Lizzie," she said in a voice that was quiet yet full of strength, "I want you to listen carefully. I know how you feel about Tom Mallory. And you know how concerned Jeff and I have been about that. I've been praying that God would show us all the truth about him." She paused, holding Lizzie's gaze with her own. "I believe He has."

Lizzie's jaw dropped, and she fought to control her quivering lower lip. "You mean you're siding with them?" She saw the pain in Judith's eyes and knew the answer.

"But I've been praying, too," Lizzie countered. "And I believe God has answered *my* prayers. Are you telling me He will answer you but not me?" She paced wildly across the room, unable to stand still a moment longer.

"Well, are you?" she demanded when Judith didn't answer.

Judith's face was pale, her gaze fixed on something in the far distance. "Lizzie —" she began.

"You're the one who told me He had a wonderful plan for my life," Lizzie broke in. "And you were right; He does. I believe Tom is part of that plan. And no matter what you or my parents think —"

"Lizzie." Quiet as it was, the tone of Judith's voice brought her up short. "I want you to gather the children together and take them home with you."

"What? Aunt Judith, you have to understand —"

"Do it now, Lizzie," Judith ordered. "Find Jeff, or send someone to get him. And send your mother over quickly." She offered a faltering smile at Lizzie's bewildered expression. "It's the baby, honey. He's coming. Do you understand, Lizzie? I need you to do these things. *Now.*"

The words finally penetrated Lizzie's brain. She helped Judith to her bed and into her nightdress, then raced out the door to obey.

Chapter 13

Two hours after returning to the ranch house, Lizzie felt as if she were ready to explode. She had gathered the three children, putting Sammy and Rose together on their gentle mare and holding little Travis securely in front of her on her own horse. Leading them home as quickly as she dared, she had been relieved to find Jeff saddling his horse. Upon hearing Lizzie's news, he climbed into the saddle and raced off without a word. Abby set out in the buggy after gathering up some supplies.

Lizzie read to the excited children, played tag and hide and seek with them, and now felt both her patience and her resources were exhausted. She settled the trio at the table in the kitchen and poured them tall glasses of milk.

"Why haven't we had any word?" she fretted to Vera, who was setting out a plate of molasses cookies. "How long does it take, anyway?"

Vera, imperturbable as always, cocked an amused eye at Lizzie. "It hasn't been all that long since Travis was born. Don't you remember how we waited all day long for news of him?"

"All day!" Lizzie fumed. "I'll go crazy if I have to stay cooped up much longer."

"Are you sure you don't have more on your mind than Judith's baby?" Vera asked with a knowing look.

Lizzie shot her a sharp glance but didn't reply. Somehow, Vera always seemed to know what was going on with members of the Bradley household, often before they were aware of it themselves.

"Why don't you go take some time for yourself?" Vera continued. "I'll keep an eye on these three until you work off some of that steam."

"Would you?" Lizzie rushed around the table to give the housekeeper a hug of gratitude. "Thanks, Vera. I wouldn't do this if I didn't really need the time alone. I'll make it up to you, I promise."

"Oh, get along now," Vera replied, giving Lizzie a good-natured swat on her behind. "Give that horse of yours a good workout and come back in a better frame of mind, that's all I ask."

Like a bird loosed from its cage, Lizzie

flew out the door. She had Dancer saddled and set out in short order. Bending low over the horse's neck, she relished the feel of the wind whipping her hair. She wished the wind could blow away the turmoil in her mind as easily.

She gave Dancer his head and exulted in his response, his long stride eating up the ground. Sooner than she thought possible, she saw the familiar outline of the cedar grove. *Their* grove, hers and Tom's. The perfect place to spend some time by herself to calm her nerves. She pulled Dancer down to a trot, then a walk, to let him cool off after their wild run.

Slipping from her saddle, she was in the process of loosening Dancer's cinch when she heard hoofbeats not far away. She was startled but not afraid. In her present mood, she wasn't afraid of anything or anyone. Just let someone try to tangle with her now!

A thought struck her and twisted her stomach into a knot. What if it was that officious Adam McKenzie, coming to spy on her? She almost hoped it was. She'd give him a piece of her mind! Peering out between the cedars, she saw not Adam's horse drawing near but Tom's.

"Tom!" she cried joyfully. She threw her

arms around his neck as soon as he dismounted.

"Whoa! Steady there," he said, trying to maintain his balance under her unexpected assault. "I saw you coming in here, but I never expected this kind of greeting." Lizzie realized just how brazen she'd been and stepped back, embarrassed. Tom's grin widened. "I'm not complaining," he continued. "In fact, I'd like to try that again." And suddenly Lizzie found herself held tightly in his arms.

She tensed, then relaxed as she warmed to the feel of his arms around her. Her own arms crept around Tom's neck again and held him fast, tightening when she felt the beat of his heart beneath her own. "Oh, Tom," she breathed. "I'm so glad you came! It's been awful these last few days."

"Miss me that much?" he asked with a cocky grin. "I think I like that." Then, seeing her troubled face, his expression sobered. "What's the matter? What's been going on?"

"Everything's the matter!" Lizzie waved her hands dramatically. Tom loosened his grip, and she strode back and forth, unable to stand still a moment longer. "It's my family — all of them. They think you're some kind of monster. They've tried to make me believe you're a gunfighter, that you're connected somehow with Billy the Kid, and that you're leading Willie and me down the path to ruin."

Tom froze in place and watched Lizzie with a guarded expression. "Where'd they get ideas like that?" he asked slowly.

"Oh, some crazy notions Uncle Jeff and Adam McKenzie got in their heads. And then when your friend came to lunch today —"

"What friend?" Tom cut in.

"He said his name was Henry Antrim." Lizzie's eyes glowed with pride while she recounted the fine things he said. "It was wonderful, Tom. Perfect timing. But then my father came home, and he thinks Henry Antrim is actually Billy the Kid."

"Your father knows?"

Lizzie went on, heedless of his words. "He and my mother had me cornered, trying to fill my head with doubts about you. But I stuck up for you, Tom. I didn't let them sway me. Even when my father said he knew about us meeting, I didn't back down a bit." She faltered a moment, noticing his shocked expression for the first time.

"You told your father about us meeting here?"

"Not to start with. That is, I don't know how he found out, but when he confronted me, I didn't deny it." She laid a trembling hand on his arm. "I couldn't deny you, Tom. I wouldn't! And he'll come around in time. Don't worry about that. I'll admit he wasn't happy when I told him how we felt about each other, but once he gets used to the idea . . ."

Tom let out a low moan and paced back and forth, raking his fingers through his hair until the dark brown strands stood on end.

"It's really all right," she told him. "I know we weren't ready to tell him about us yet, but . . ." Her voice trailed off at the look on Tom's face.

He stopped his pacing and took her by the shoulders. "Lizzie," he began in a husky voice. She looked at him wonderingly, trustingly. He held her gaze for a moment, then averted his eyes. He cleared his throat and started over. "You're a wonderful girl, Lizzie." Her heart felt as though it would pound right through her chest. The moment had come at last — he was about to propose! "Way too good for the likes of me."

Her heart melted while she watched him struggle to find the right words. "You don't have to go through all this," she whispered. "I know what you're trying to say."

"I don't think so." He laughed bitterly and drew a long breath, then framed her face with his hands. "Lizzie, there is no 'us.'"

She smiled reassuringly and shook her head. "It's all right. No matter what they say, I believe in you, Tom." A bold idea struck her. "In fact, I'll leave with you right now. Once we're married, they'll have to —"

"Hold on, there!" The alarmed note in his voice stopped her as effectively as a dousing with cold water. "Listen to me, Lizzie, and listen good." One glance at her bewildered face made him groan again.

"Look, honey, I never meant to hurt you. You're a sweet girl and we've had a lot of fun together." Lizzie felt like she had stepped off a cliff into empty space. This wasn't going at all the way it was supposed to.

Tom looked at her with pleading eyes, begging her to understand. "But that's all that it's been, fun. A good time."

"A good time?" Lizzie echoed hollowly. "But, Tom, you kissed me! You let me think —"

"Hold on there. Whatever you thought

was all in your own mind, not mine." He scrubbed his hands together. "I like women, Lizzie. I always have. And they've always liked me." He shrugged, and his lips curled up in a self-deprecating grin that twisted at her heart.

"You mean you've done this . . . with other women? It didn't mean anything special to you?"

Tom's grin faded, and he shifted from one foot to the other. "Come on, Lizzie, you're making too big a thing out of this. Sure I've kissed other women. I've done a lot more than kiss some of them, too." His voice took on an angry tone. "But you're such an innocent, I couldn't go any further with you. I do have some scruples, you know."

Lizzie couldn't answer. Without another word, Tom grabbed his horse's reins and swung into the saddle.

He paused at the edge of the grove and turned to her one last time. "I'm leaving now. Knowing how your father feels, I don't think I'll be welcome here much longer." His voice grew rough with irritation. "It's time you grew up, Lizzie. Quit acting like I've done something terrible. I didn't do a thing to hurt you, not really. And you never know," he continued, the familiar heart-stopping grin beginning to tug at the corners of his mouth, "I may have done you a favor by waking you up a bit. You may wind up thanking me for this after all." He spurred his mount and loped off toward the distant hills.

Lizzie stood frozen in place. Finally she moved one stiff leg forward, then the other, until she halted just inside the protective shelter of the trees. Standing with one hand braced against the trunk of a small cedar, she watched numbly as Tom's figure dwindled to a speck in the distance, then topped a low hill to disappear from her life forever.

Chapter 14

Lizzie turned and made her stumbling way back to the fallen log. Their log. She looked again at the places she had treasured. The promises she thought they held had turned out to be empty, and she felt as if their very existence mocked her.

She clung to the numbness, wrapping herself in its folds as if it were a protective cocoon. If she waited long enough, surely this would turn out to be nothing more than a bad dream. But never, never in a million years would she have dreamed Tom would betray her trust, then ride away.

Lizzie could feel her protective armor cracking, and she fought against it. If she could preserve this blessed lack of feeling, she might somehow live through this moment. But the first pricks of pain skirted their way through the fragile shell and opened the way for other, stronger shafts of anguish that assured her this was no dream but bitter reality.

Tom's words came back to dance through her mind, tormenting her thoughts. What was it he'd said? "Quit acting like I've done something terrible. I never meant to hurt you." If only he knew!

Lizzie's legs began to tremble so that she could barely stand. Then they gave way altogether, and she pitched forward onto her knees and buried her face in her lap. How could she have been so foolish?

She pressed her hands over her eyes, trying to blot out the sight of those places she had thought so special. Despite her efforts, her mind pitilessly replayed every memory of every moment she and Tom had spent together.

Lizzie writhed with humiliation as those scenes unfolded. Looking at them with the eyes of her painful new knowledge, she could see how naive she must have seemed to Tom, whose worldly experience vastly outweighed her own. How he must have laughed, seeing how easily she had been duped! She had yielded to everything he asked of her, would have run off at a single word from him, she remembered with mortification. And those moments she deemed so precious never meant anything to him at all.

Lizzie rocked back and forth, her breath coming out in helpless little whimpers that grew into racking sobs. Knowing she was utterly alone, Lizzie gave way to her feelings and wailed aloud as she poured out her pain, her grief, her shame.

Adam McKenzie rode in a slow loop that would bring him back to ranch headquarters soon after dark. What a whirlwind day this had turned out to be! He thought he would be glad to see Tom Mallory's true character unmasked. But after Charles's revelation and the following confrontation between him and Lizzie, then Jeff's rapid departure to see to the birth of his fourth child, Adam decided he'd had enough emotional turmoil for one day.

He volunteered to look over the area Charles and Jeff wanted to fence, knowing it would take him the rest of the day to finish the job and welcoming the solitude it offered. After what he'd gone through, Adam felt he was due for some peace and quiet.

Inspecting the area meant a fair amount of physical exertion but involved little thought, just what he needed to calm his spirit and clear his brain. The lengthy ride gave him plenty of time to do some serious praying, too, something Adam was grateful for.

He leaned back in his saddle, more relaxed than he had been in days, and enjoyed his horse's smooth, even gait. When the bay's ears pricked up and pointed straight ahead, it took a moment to register in Adam's mind. Then he snapped out of his reverie and looked to see what had caught the animal's attention.

In the distance, a lone rider emerged from a stand of trees. The rider halted and turned his mount slightly, as though he meant to turn back, then wheeled the horse around and headed south at a gallop.

Adam stopped and tried to puzzle it out. As far as he knew, no Bradley riders should have been in the area, and no one else had any call to be there. Of course, it could be a drifter who found a shady spot for an afternoon rest. But why pause and turn back? And why ride away in such a hurry?

Moreover, the outline of horse and rider bore a striking resemblance to Tom Mallory, and Adam could see no reason for him to be stopping there. No good reason, that is. But with Mallory, who could tell?

It bore checking out, Adam thought. He nudged his horse into a trot, then a lope.

Adam didn't like mysteries. He preferred things to be honest and open, and there had been far too many things lately that had been anything but. He'd be glad to satisfy his curiosity on this point so easily.

He slowed again as he neared the trees, looking for tracks and any other telltale signs that might help him grasp the situation. He cut across the trail of the other horse and felt a grim satisfaction when he recognized the tracks of Mallory's mount. He had come along here, paused for a moment or two, then continued toward the trees. *Finding a quiet spot to practice his gunslinging?*

The bay halted of its own accord at the same moment Adam heard the sound. An eerie wail, rising and falling, only to rise again, sounding like an animal in torment. Not daring to speculate on what he might find, he jabbed his spurs into his horse's flanks and headed into the trees at a gallop.

Adam pulled his horse to a sliding stop when he spotted another horse standing head down in the clearing. *Dancer?* He swung around frantically, and his heart stood still at the sight of a disheveled Lizzie crumpled in a heap in the dust, howling out her misery like a lost soul.

He froze for a moment, fearing the worst. Then he leapt toward her and gathered her in his arms. "Lizzie, sweetheart, what is it?" he murmured gently, all the while thinking, *Mallory! If he's harmed her, he'll regret the day he was born!*

He pressed her head against his chest with one hand and stroked her hair, comforting her as he would a frightened child. To his great relief, Lizzie didn't resist his embrace but leaned against his shoulder and continued to weep.

Adam settled Lizzie into his lap, feeling the warmth of her body, feeling it quiver against him. He crooned endearments in her ear, not knowing whether she heard, but hoping the soothing sounds would calm her. The sweetness of this proximity was something Adam would have wanted to prolong had it been under happier circumstances. Now, though, it was vital to find out just what was wrong before Tom Mallory gained too much of a head start.

"Shh, honey, settle down. I need to talk to you," he whispered, smoothing moist wisps of hair away from her forehead with his fingertips. "Can you hear me, Lizzie?" Sobs continued to rack her body, and her shoulders jerked convulsively, although her cries were diminishing in volume.

Adam groaned inwardly, even as he tightened his hold on her. *Lizzie, my love, I can't stand seeing you like this. I promise you, if Mallory has harmed you in any way, I'll take care of that sorry piece of trash myself!*

Finally, only a few pitiful moans escaped her lips, and while her breath continued to come in jerky gasps, it seemed to Adam that most of the tumult had passed. Breathing more easily himself, he loosened his hold on Lizzie, rocking gently as he cradled her in his arms.

The fervent wish that she were there of her own accord was immediately followed by a mental tongue-lashing. Adam berated himself for enjoying a situation that cost Lizzie so much. And what that cost might be was something that needed to be determined quickly, he reminded himself, before the miscreant had time to complete his getaway.

Adam put a finger under Lizzie's chin and tilted her head back gently. It took a moment for her eyes, still blurred by tears, to focus on his face and another moment before she seemed fully aware of who he was. When awareness of his presence registered on her features, she ducked her head again and laid it trustingly against his chest. Adam thrilled to the knowledge that she did this of her own volition, and his hand trembled as he tenderly wiped the tears from her sodden cheeks.

How he'd love to stay like this, enjoying her nearness and being her source of comfort! But duty reared its stern head and reminded him that he needed information and needed it now.

How on earth do I ask her? He felt a momentary panic. It ought to be her father talking to her like this or at least Jeff. *Lord, You're going to have to give me the words and the strength, because I can't do this one on my own.*

"Lizzie?" he asked tentatively. "Can you hear me now?" She swiveled slightly in his lap, raising her face to meet his. Her lips still quivered, but he was relieved to see that her breathing had steadied.

She nodded slowly, her eyes dull. "Yes, Adam. I hear you."

Adam swallowed and tried to work some moisture into his suddenly dry mouth. "When I was riding up, I saw someone leaving here. It looked like — like Mallory. Was it?"

Lizzie's lips quivered even more, and Adam could feel the tremor that ran through her body. "Was it?" he repeated gently.

She lowered her eyes. "Yes. It was him."

Adam drew a ragged breath. "Lizzie, I have to ask you this. Lord knows I don't want to, but I need to know. Did he . . . did he hurt you?"

Lizzie buried her face in her hands, and Adam's heart sank like a stone. She heaved a great sigh and raised her face once more, still avoiding his eyes. "No, Adam," she whispered. "Not in the way you mean."

Adam tried not to let the surge of relief show in his voice. If she hadn't been harmed physically, it was obvious that something had happened to reduce her to this state, and he meant to tread softly so as not to cause her more pain.

"Then what is it?" he asked, taking advantage of the moment and daring to encircle her in his arms once more. "You don't go to pieces like this for nothing."

Her brittle laugh shocked him. "Don't I?" she asked bitterly. "You pulled me off of Willie just the other day, remember? And you saw that scene in my father's office, as I recall. The one where I made a complete fool of myself standing up for T–Tom." She managed to get the last words out just before her face crumpled. She pressed one hand against her lips.

"There's nothing wrong with standing

up for what you believe in," Adam said, searching frantically for the right words to offer her.

Lizzie battled for control before she could speak again. "There is when what you believe in is based on a lie."

"You mean Mallory —"

"Tom's gone," Lizzie stated flatly. "Gone for good. I was a fool, Adam. A fool, pure and simple."

"No, Lizzie. Never that. If you had feelings for Mallory and thought they were returned, it was his doing, not yours." Her silence gave Adam the boldness to continue. "Maybe he's never met a woman like you before, someone who's loving and good. He didn't have the sense to realize what he had and treasure it." His arms tightened around her just a fraction. "If anyone's a fool, Lizzie, it's him, not you."

She tilted her head and looked him fully in the eyes as if searching the depths of his soul. She nodded slowly, apparently satisfied with what she saw. "Thank you, Adam. I believe you mean that." Her lips curved briefly in a tremulous smile. "I'm only sorry I can't agree with you."

Adam's senses reeled at the intensity of her gaze. For once he held Lizzie Bradley's attention and held it completely.

He held Lizzie herself, for that matter, he reminded himself with wonder. The golden hair flowed across his hands in a shimmering wave, and he longed to twine his fingers through its silken strands. Her breath brushed softly against his face.

Looking at the pale pink lips mere inches from his own, Adam wanted more than anything to stop their trembling with his own firm lips, giving her a pledge that as long as he was around, she would never be hurt like that again.

The moment held, then was broken when Lizzie drew back and scrubbed her hands against her face, suddenly looking more like a lost little girl than a desirable woman.

Probably for the best, Lord. If I started kissing her, it'd be awfully hard to quit.

He helped Lizzie to her feet, and after she took a few unsteady steps, he boldly scooped her up and carried her. She lay unresisting, a welcome weight in his arms. He reluctantly set her down next to Dancer.

"I don't know what I would have done if you hadn't come along, Adam," she said softly, looking up at him through still-damp lashes while he checked the cinch and gathered the reins for her.

She laid her hand on his arm, and a wild thought jolted through him. After all the years of keeping his distance, to have her so near now was overwhelming. Could he dare believe she had feelings for him, too? His heart soared, feeling the first faint stirring of hope. Maybe now was the time to tell her how he felt.

"I want to thank you," she continued, as he tried to marshal his thoughts.

"Lizzie —" he began.

"Having you hold me like that . . ."

Adam's throat constricted, and he could hardly believe his ears. Was she telling him she'd enjoyed being held? "I've been waiting for a long time for the chance to —"

"I can't tell you how wonderful it was."

Wonderful didn't fully describe it for Adam. He would use words like *heavenly* or *stupendous*. This was going to be easier than he'd thought.

"Lizzie, what I'm trying to say is —"

"It was just like having my father hold me when I was little."

Adam's heart, which had been spiraling into the clouds, plummeted back to the dusty earth with a resounding thud.

"Your father?" he echoed.

Lizzie nodded, her earnest gaze fixed on Adam's. "My mother was very ill when I was a little girl. A few times I got so scared at the thought of losing her that I just fell apart. My father would take me in his lap and hold me and rock me — just like you did — and somehow I knew things were going to be all right."

"Your father," Adam repeated.

"And Uncle Jeff helped, too, sometimes," she added, summoning up a brave smile. "My two favorite men. I guess that almost makes you family, doesn't it, Adam? Kind of like a big brother."

Adam stared in silence, feeling like someone had just poured ice water over him. He shook his head, trying to clear it. *You idiot! And Lizzie thinks* she *built something up out of nothing!*

He grabbed her, none too gently, at her waist, boosted her unceremoniously into the saddle, and handed her the reins. Lizzie stared back at him uncertainly.

"You'd better head for home," he said, slapping Dancer on the rump. "I've got work to finish before dark."

Chapter 15

Lizzie neared the ranch house, flopping loosely in her saddle. Her father would have criticized her horsemanship, calling it sloppy, but right now she didn't care. Her world had turned upside down in the space of a few hours, and something as insignificant as her riding ability wasn't important at the moment.

Nothing seemed important just now. She couldn't remember a time in her life when she'd gone through so many conflicting emotions in such a short time. The hope, the joy that filled her life so recently, had given way to an aching emptiness, and Lizzie didn't know how she was going to cope with that. She was only nineteen, she reflected. How could she exist another fifty years or so, feeling the way she did now?

How could I have been so blind? The question had plagued her all during the ride home. *I thought he loved me! How can I ever trust my own judgment again?*

The house and outbuildings came into sight, and a wave of depression swept over her. She would have to face her family soon. As if the humiliation she had just experienced weren't bad enough, the hardest part was just beginning.

Bitter thoughts swirled through her mind. *After all the fine things I've said about Tom and our "love," I'll never be able to hold up my head again.* How could any of them ever look at her without remembering what a fool she'd been? Her father would hardly be able to wait to say "I told you so."

Adam hadn't, though. And considering that he had seen Tom's true character early on, that surprised her. But he'd only held her and comforted her and seemed more concerned about her feelings than her stupidity.

A tiny frown creased her brow. He'd been so tender and caring right up until she was ready to mount Dancer. Then he'd all but shoved her up on the saddle and sent her on her way. What happened? She'd only tried to thank him for his kindness, and it seemed to anger him.

Apparently she'd misread Adam, too. More evidence, if she'd needed more, that she wasn't any judge of men.

Dancer ambled by the corrals, and Lizzie braced herself, hoping against hope that she wouldn't meet anyone until she had a chance to pull herself together. That hope shattered the moment she led Dancer into the barn and encountered Willie. With one sweeping glance, he took in her distraught appearance and blurted out, "What happened to you?"

Lizzie pressed her lips together, wishing he would go away. Willie followed her and watched her begin to groom Dancer. "Where have you been? You missed all the excitement."

"I've had enough excitement of my own, thanks."

"Well, there'll probably be more to come tonight, with all three kids staying over here."

All three kids? What . . . With a start, she remembered she'd left her cousins in Vera's care, not intending to be gone long. And here it was, almost dark. Her shoulders slumped. One more proof of her flightiness.

She closed Dancer in his stall and tossed him a flake of hay. "Why are they staying?"

Willie stared at her as though she'd sprouted an extra head. "The baby, remember? Everyone thought Jeff and Judith would be better off spending the first night with just them and the baby, instead of having all the other kids jumping in and trying to help."

"Oh, the baby's here? That's nice." Now she'd have to spend time taking care of the children instead of hiding out in her room.

"What's wrong with you, Sis? I thought you'd be as excited as the kids are." Willie peered at her more closely in the gathering dusk. "You've got that kind of faraway look on your face, like when you've just seen Tom." He perked up like a hound on a scent. "Is that it? Is Tom back? You've seen him, haven't you? Hey, that's great! I've been practicing, and he's really gonna be surprised when —"

Lizzie stiffened under the onslaught of questions. "He's gone, Willie."

It took a moment for her words to sink in. "You mean he had to leave again? What for? When's he coming back?"

"He isn't." Her hands clenched and released, balling the fabric of her riding skirt into a mass of wrinkles. "He left this afternoon, and he won't be coming back. Ever." Her throat felt thick and the prick of tears stung her eyelids.

Willie threw up his hands in disgust. "For crying out loud, Sis! What did you do to run him off — throw yourself at him?" The justice of that remark was more than Lizzie could bear. She ran sobbing to the house, where she managed to evade her small cousins and barricade herself in her room.

Dropping to her knees beside her bed, she buried her face in the coverlet and gave vent to her emotions. As the sobs shook her shoulders, her heart cried out to God. *I don't understand what's happening. I prayed; You know I did. Aunt Judith says You always hear our prayers, but what happened this time? I thought I heard from You, and look how wrong I was! You're supposed to be the hope of Your people. You're supposed to work all things together for good, and I thought that's what You were doing. Now everything's falling apart, and I don't know how I'll ever know whether I'm doing the right thing again.*

She drew a shuddering breath, and the question sprang forth from the depths of her soul: *What's wrong with me?*

Footsteps sounded in the hallway, and a rapid tapping at the door brought her to her feet. Mindless of the damage to the coverlet, she used it to mop her face and brushed her hair back with both hands.

"What is it?" she called, her voice sounding strained and unnatural.

"About time you got back," came Vera's cheery voice.

"I'm coming to take over with the children," Lizzie said, hurrying to smooth her clothing into place. She opened the door to find Vera standing there alone.

"Don't worry about them," Vera told her. "The little scamps finally wore themselves out, and I put them to bed nearly an hour ago."

"I'm sorry! I didn't mean to go off and leave you so long."

"It's not the first time I've had to deal with rambunctious youngsters." Vera gave her a reassuring pat on the shoulder. "I just wanted to let you know there's a cold supper waiting in the kitchen. Things have been in such a flurry today, I decided it would be better to let you all help yourselves when you had a chance."

"Thanks. That was a good idea," Lizzie said, thinking guiltily of the extra responsibility that had been heaped on Vera's shoulders this day. "Willie said the baby has come," she ventured, following Vera to the kitchen. "What's his name?"

" 'His' name is Susannah." Vera chuckled.

"It's a girl?" The news momentarily shocked Lizzie out of her despondency. "But Aunt Judith —"

"Was mistaken," Vera finished for her. "But that's not to say she isn't thrilled. And from the way your mother described Jeff strutting around, it sounds like he's not too disappointed, either. As for Rose, she's floating on air at having another girl in the family. Says it's about time things were evened up a bit."

Lizzie's mouth curved slightly, in spite of herself. "I'm glad for them." Then she frowned. "Do you mean Mama's back already? I thought she planned to stay for a couple of days, at least."

"That was the plan," Vera agreed. "But she said Jeff told her he'd done this with three babies already; he figured he was capable of handling things with this one, too. Your mother's getting a bite to eat right now." She paused outside the kitchen door.

Lizzie stopped in her tracks. "Go on ahead. I'll be there in a minute."

Vera raised a quizzical eyebrow but complied. Lizzie leaned against the wall for support. There would be no postponing the interview with her mother now. She inhaled deeply and squared her shoulders. She was as prepared as she'd ever be. *Time to get it over with.*

Lizzie found she wasn't prepared, though, when she met not only her mother's inquisitive gaze, but her father's and Willie's as well. Her step faltered, but she forced herself to move to the sideboard and begin filling her plate with a calm she didn't feel.

Abby barely paused to acknowledge Lizzie's entrance before turning back to Charles and Willie. "She has Judith's blond hair and lots of it. I don't think I've ever seen so much hair on a newborn! She's quiet, too. Seems like a calm little thing."

"That'll be a nice change," Charles said, grinning.

"Isn't that the truth?" Abby agreed with a laugh. "They're about due for a break. But wait 'til you see her, Charles. She's such a beautiful baby!"

Charles regarded his wife with fond amusement. "I don't believe you've ever seen a baby you didn't think was absolutely beautiful," he teased. "Is there such a child?"

"I guess not," Abby admitted. "At least not to me." The look that passed between them made Lizzie's breath catch in her throat. It was a look that spoke of a relationship filled with understanding and trust. The kind she had thought she'd found with Tom.

Charles shifted his gaze to his daughter. "And what have you been up to? Vera says you were gone quite awhile."

The abrupt question caught Lizzie off guard, and she took her time answering.

"I needed to be alone for a bit," she said quietly. "So I went for a ride."

Willie snorted. "Alone, right?" he sneered.

Charles's brows drew together. "And what does that mean?"

"Nothing —" Lizzie started to reply, but Willie cut in.

"She may have left alone and come back alone," he said, "but somewhere along the way she ran into Tom, then she ran him off."

Abby took in a quick breath. She and Charles turned astonished eyes on their daughter. Charles's face looked like a thundercloud. "You saw him again? After what I told you?"

Whatever Lizzie had imagined this scene would be like, the reality was a hundred times worse. "Yes, I saw him," she answered in a voice that shook. "But it wasn't planned. He happened to see me when he was on his way back home, and he stopped to talk to me."

"Just talk?" The suspicion in her father's tone made Lizzie flinch.

"Yes." Only a few hours earlier, she would have bristled at the implication and leaped to Tom's defense. Now, she found herself barely able to meet her father's eyes. "He . . . he wanted to tell me he was leaving."

"For where? What's he up to?"

Lizzie closed her eyes. "I don't know where he's going. I only know he isn't coming back."

Silence greeted her announcement, followed by Willie's muttered comment: "Yeah. Thanks to her."

"What are you suggesting she did?" Charles turned on his son.

Willie shrugged uncomfortably, as though he sensed he'd pushed too far. "I don't know, but she must have done something."

Abby laid her hand on Lizzie's arm. "Are you all right, dear?" Her tone showed concern, but Lizzie could see the relief in her mother's eyes.

Charles opened his mouth but closed it again at a wave of Abby's hand. Lizzie bit her lower lip, wishing she could control the quaver in her voice.

"I'll be fine," she said, knowing that it wasn't true at all. After the things she had said and done — after being totally convinced she knew God's direction for her life — she didn't see how she could ever be all right again.

Her father spoke in a softer voice. "Of course you'll be all right. You're a good girl, Lizzie, and you have a lot to look forward to."

Lizzie's eyes blurred with tears. She wasn't good at all. She was an idiot, a ninny who couldn't trust her own judgment.

If she didn't change the subject now, she knew she'd break down in front of all of them, and she couldn't bear that. "Are the children supposed to go home tomorrow? I'll take them back to meet little Susannah," she said with forced brightness.

"That's fine, dear," her mother answered. "Why don't you go to bed now and get a good night's rest; you've had a long day." Before Lizzie could answer, the kitchen door burst open and Bert stumbled inside.

Charles leaped to his feet and hurried to the cowboy's side. "What is it?" he asked.

Looking at Bert's ashen face, Lizzie held her breath, knowing she was about to hear something horrible.

"It's Dan Peterson." Bert's breath came in quick gasps. He leaned against the counter for support. "He was coming out of Farley's store in town and he was shot, right there in the street. Happened about an hour ago."

Lizzie felt the color drain from her face and glanced at Willie. He looked as stricken as she felt. They had known Mr. Peterson since early childhood, and their father had often jokingly accused him of spoiling them when he had brought them candy and spent countless hours telling them stories. Lizzie knew Dan Peterson to be a kind, generous man who had never hurt a single person in his life.

"Is he . . ." She couldn't bring herself to say the word.

Bert shook his head, raking his fingers through his hair. "Doc thinks he'll pull through, but it'll take time. He was hurt pretty bad."

"Why Dan?" Charles rasped. "How did it happen?"

Bert spread his hands wide. "There wasn't any reason for it, boss. None at all. A couple of yahoos were shooting at signs.

Dan walked out right smack in the middle of it." He gulped in a breath and cleared his throat. "One of 'em even had the gall to laugh and say it was Dan's own fault. Said Dan shouldn't have got in the line of fire."

"Who did it, Bert?" Willie rose from his seat, his young face stern and pale. "Do they know?"

"Yeah, they do." Bert looked down and studied the toes of his boots. "One of 'em was Billy the Kid. No one recognized his friend, but he was medium height, slim build, brown hair. About Billy's age." He looked up at Charles with somber eyes. "Looks like Lincoln County's trouble has become ours, don't it?"

"It looks like it's come all too close to home," Charles agreed, his gaze fixed on his children. Willie sank back into his chair as though his legs would no longer support him.

The room swam before Lizzie, and she left without a word, knowing she might faint if she stayed a moment longer. Once in her room, she threw her clothes off into an untidy heap and sought the sweet oblivion of sleep.

Chapter 16

Abby's birthday dawned bright and clear. The moment Lizzie opened her eyes, she knew it was going to be a perfect day. As far as the weather was concerned, anyway. Her own spirits would have been more in tune with an overcast sky filled with lowering clouds.

Time supposedly brought healing. But the two weeks following Tom's departure hadn't done a thing to ease her pain or restore her confidence. She awoke each morning to a dull throb of hopelessness that didn't dissipate as the day wore on.

Lizzie avoided contact with the rest of the family as much as possible, unable to face either their censure or their pity. She even turned her mirror to the wall so as not to have to face her own reflection.

This day, though, she knew she owed it to her mother to present as bright a face as possible, so she swiveled the mirror back around before she began dressing her hair.

Lizzie reached for her hairbrush, then halted with her hand outstretched, staring at the forlorn creature peering back at her. Hollow eyes gazed listlessly into her own. Her skin stretched tautly over her cheekbones, and her hair hung dull and limp. No wonder she had caught worried looks from her parents and Vera the past few days.

Lizzie drew the brush through her hair again and again, trying to restore some of its normal luster. In the end it lay neatly over her shoulders but lacked its customary sheen. It would just have to do, she thought as she swept it back and tied it in place with a sky-blue ribbon.

She slipped out of her nightdress and selected a matching blue dress with more ruffles and flounces than she ordinarily wore, hoping its cheerful hue might give her wan cheeks more life. It helped a little but not much, Lizzie decided, surveying her appearance in the mirror once more.

I look like I've been sick for a month. She pinched her cheeks and bit her lips to bring out some color.

Vera rapped on the door and stuck her head inside the room. "Well, look who's up and dressed," she said cheerfully. "I brought your breakfast on a tray since it's a special occasion."

Lizzie felt a surge of gratitude for Vera's thoughtfulness, followed by a twinge of guilt when she remembered how she had avoided Vera the past two weeks.

"Thank you," she said, attempting a smile. "But I'm not the birthday girl, remember?"

"Doesn't matter." Vera swept in and set down the tray with her usual efficiency, then turned to survey Lizzie with a practiced eye. "It's an improvement," she said, giving a satisfied nod. "It'll do a lot for your mother's peace of mind. Thanks, Lizzie. We can always count on you in a crunch." She gave Lizzie's shoulders a quick squeeze and was gone.

Lizzie stared at the closed door, openmouthed. Was it possible Vera didn't despise her after all? She picked at the fluffy scrambled eggs and discovered she had an appetite for the first time in days.

With no other plans for the day, Lizzie found herself with time on her hands. She wandered down to the barn and went directly to Dancer's stall. The gelding pushed his head over the half door and whickered a welcome.

"Hello, fella." Lizzie stroked his glossy neck lovingly, mindful of her dress and the need to keep it clean. "I haven't paid much attention to you lately, have I?"

Dancer nuzzled her hair in answer, and she pushed his head away with a gentle hand. "Not now, boy. I have to look presentable today. But tomorrow I'll wear something more suitable and give you the best rubdown you've ever had to make up for it. And we'll start going out again soon, I promise."

The scuff of boots behind her made her turn. Adam stood there, as if hesitant about whether to enter the aisle. Lizzie watched him warily. Adam had come to her rescue when she thought her world had ended, but then he had ridden away. Apparently his solicitous concern was only commiseration for her tears. Once he sorted through what had actually happened, he was as disgusted with her as everyone else. After all, he left her almost as abruptly as Tom had.

Lizzie found his actions thoroughly confusing. But then, she was having trouble understanding even her own feelings. Why, for instance, should the knowledge that Adam McKenzie held her in low regard bring such a sharp pang of regret?

"Hello," she faltered. "Am I in your way?"

Adam blinked as if just waking up, and a slow smile spread across his face. "Sorry. It's just that I'm not usually met by such a lovely sight when I come in to feed in the morning."

Lizzie felt the heat wash across her face and knew it must be as pink as the roses her mother planted near the front door. The aisle seemed to have shrunk somehow, leaving barely enough room for the two of them. Was he serious or making fun of her? Given his baffling behavior two weeks ago, how could she possibly know? Better to take the safe road and not make any rash assumptions that might embarrass her again. Hurrying to get past him, she murmured, "I'd better get back to the house."

The aisle truly had shrunk, she decided when she attempted to squeeze by Adam without brushing her dress against the wall. He turned sideways at the same time she did, and they stood face to face, mere inches apart.

Lizzie wondered if a thunderstorm was brewing. There was that same tingling feeling in the air, raising bumps all along her arms. Adam seemed to sense it, too, for his dark gaze was fixed on hers, and he stood as if rooted to the spot.

Lizzie recovered first. *Here I am, about*

to make a fool of myself again. What must he be thinking? Aloud, she said, "Excuse me, I need to go."

Adam watched Lizzie leave and tried to get his heart to slow back down to its normal rate. *Idiot! Every time you get a chance to talk to her, you freeze up like a block of ice.*

He shook his head, reliving the encounter. Every nerve in his body had reacted to her nearness, and it left him breathless. He could have sworn she felt it, too. But he would have sworn she'd looked on him as something more than a brother when she had nestled in his arms that day two weeks earlier.

He went about his chores, kicking himself mentally and wishing he could find someone with good, sturdy boots who could do a more thorough job of it.

Jeff, Judith, and all four children arrived shortly after the noon meal. The family gathered in the living room, where they could watch Abby open her gifts and fuss over baby Susannah.

Lizzie looked anxiously at Judith, hoping that with all the excitement of the new baby, she hadn't forgotten the precious quilt. A reassuring wink from her aunt put her mind at rest, and she settled into a wingback chair, trying to give the appearance of enjoying the festivities.

Rose, Sammy, and Travis presented their family's gift first, bearing it importantly, as befitting their mature status. Abby oohed and aahed over the job they had done on the wrapping and carefully opened the box to reveal a delicate china tea set.

"We helped pack it," Travis volunteered. "But not Susannah. She's too little." The twins nodded in solemn agreement.

"Thank you all," Abby said, gathering the three in a big hug. "It's wonderful." She smiled at Jeff and Judith, including them in her thanks as well.

Willie's offering came next, and his mother expressed delight at the tortoiseshell comb and mirror he gave her. He received her thanks with a grateful smile. The unwarranted shooting of Dan Peterson seemed to have awakened Willie. Little by little, his sunny disposition had returned, much to the relief of the entire family.

Lizzie fidgeted in her chair. Would her mother really like the quilt? She almost wished she had substituted something else for it instead, some trinket that would please her mother without making Lizzie feel so vulnerable. Maybe no one would notice if she didn't present the quilt to her mother. Or if they did, perhaps they would assume she had been too distraught this last couple of weeks to remember to get a gift. Maybe it was better to be seen as thoughtless than an object of pity.

Charles glanced around. "I guess I'm next." He handed Abby a small white box. "Here you are, dear. Many happy returns of the day."

She opened it with care and stared for a moment at what lay inside. "Charles, it's beautiful," she breathed, lifting from the folds of paper a delicately crafted gold pin fashioned in the shape of an oak leaf. Crystal drops shone in the corners of her eyes as she gazed at her husband.

"I picked it up on my last trip to Santa Fe," he said, obviously pleased with his gift's success. "I'm glad you like it."

"You knew I would," Abby told him. She pinned it on her dress. "Thank you so much." She gave his hand a tender squeeze, and a look passed between them that made Lizzie feel the rest of the group was intruding upon a special moment meant only for them. She tried to ignore a stab of envy.

Abby gave a happy sigh. "It's been a wonderful birthday. Thank you all very much." Lizzie tried to ignore Judith's quizzical look. After seeing all those wonderful gifts, she couldn't bear it if her own was a disappointment.

"Shall we go into the dining room for some refreshment?" Abby took Charles's arm and prepared to lead the way. She looked questioningly at Judith, who was clearing her throat repeatedly.

Getting no response from Lizzie, Judith took it upon herself to speak. "I think you have one more present, Abby. Jeff, would you bring it in from the wagon?"

Jeff left the room with a grin on his face, and Lizzie sank farther down in the chair, wishing she could pass right through the cushion, the floor, and into the earth itself.

Willie held the door open for Jeff, who maneuvered a mysterious bundle wrapped in brown paper through the doorway and held it out to Abby. She accepted it with a smile but looked curiously at Judith. "Another one?" she asked.

"This one is from your daughter," Judith replied.

Abby's eyes shone with delight and she beamed at Lizzie. "Thank you, dear," she said.

"Better wait 'til you open it before you get too excited," Willie muttered, earning a reproving look from his father.

Lizzie held her breath as she watched her mother tear the paper away. Abby stopped with her hands in midair and stared at the bright colors of the quilt. Silence filled the room as she touched the fabric tentatively, tracing the lovingly stitched design. She looked first at Judith, then Lizzie, her eyes filled with wonder. "You made this, Lizzie?"

Lizzie nodded, hoping against hope she hadn't let her mother down again.

"But how? When?"

"I asked Aunt Judith to show me how. We made it at her house, and she helped a lot. I wanted to do something special for you . . . ," she added, trailing off lamely.

"And you have." Her mother's eyes glowed with happiness. "Charles, just look at this!" She spread out the quilt, carefully smoothing the folds. Everyone gathered around, with Jeff and Judith keeping their eager threesome at a safe distance. Lizzie's handiwork was duly inspected and approved.

Abby slipped away from the group and came over to kneel by Lizzie's chair. "It's beautiful," she told her. "But I still don't know how you managed it. How long did it take you?"

"We've been working on it for months," Lizzie admitted. "We got it finished just before Susannah was born." She flinched inwardly, remembering what else occurred on that fateful day.

"And you kept it a secret all this time?" Abby shook her head, smiling. "I don't know why that surprises me, though. It's just the sort of thoughtful thing you'd do." She slipped her arms around her astonished daughter and held her close. "Thank you, Lizzie," she whispered. "I'll treasure it always."

"I'm glad you like it, Mama," Lizzie responded, returning her mother's embrace. She felt so good, so loved. If only she could measure up to her mother's opinion of her!

Chapter 17

"Are you ready for the picnic, Lizzie?" Rose's eyes shone with excitement, and she bounced from one foot to the other in anticipation.

Lizzie sighed and tried to summon up a smile for her cousin's benefit. She tried to opt out of attending the annual church function, but her parents insisted they needed her help to keep an eye on Jeff's three oldest youngsters. Susannah and her parents needed some time alone together, they reasoned, and with all the excitement the picnic would bring, it would take every available person to make sure the children didn't get into too much mischief.

Lizzie wasn't sure whether the need for her help was real or a manufactured reason to get her away from the ranch and out of her doldrums. She suspected the latter, and while she appreciated her parents' concern, she wished they would leave her to her own devices. Especially when it involved a church activity. Church was one place Lizzie simply didn't belong.

Right now Lizzie didn't feel like she and God were on especially good terms. She had tried to forge ahead in spiritual knowledge. She'd read her Bible and discovered verses she thought applied to her, and look what happened. God might talk to others, but He obviously didn't communicate with Lizzie Bradley.

Rose's insistent bouncing brought Lizzie back to the moment at hand. She gathered her cousins together, feeling something like a mother hen when they followed her out to the wagon, where Vera efficiently loaded them and the baskets of food. "You're ready to go," she announced, smiling.

Lizzie's parents emerged from the house, and Charles boosted Abby to the wagon seat before taking his place beside her and clucking to the horses. Lizzie sat in back with the children and waved good-bye to Vera, who declared that her old bones weren't up to all that jouncing around anymore.

Several of the cowboys rode alongside the wagon, ready to take advantage of any opportunity to socialize with their far-flung neighbors. Lizzie glanced around but didn't see Adam among them. *Just as well.* She breathed a little easier. Ever since their encounter at the grove, and especially since their meeting in the barn, she found his presence unnerving.

She leaned back against the sideboard and closed her eyes. The light breeze played with loose strands of her hair and tugged at her full skirt. The constant rocking of the wagon lulled her into a half-doze, broken only by the excited chatter of Rose, Sam, and Travis, who saw this outing as a high point of their existence.

Lizzie sighed, adrift in her own world. If only her life could be as simple as theirs! Lost in her thoughts, it seemed only a brief time until they arrived at the picnic grounds. The children scrambled over the tailgate even before the wagon came to a stop, with Abby's admonitions to stay close and behave apparently falling on deaf ears. Lizzie helped carry their baskets to the waiting table and tried to avoid conversation with the friendly but inquisitive older women who were organizing the food.

When her mother handed her a blanket and told her to find a place for them all to sit, Lizzie seized the opportunity for escape gratefully. She spread the blanket on the ground a distance away from the others, telling herself the children would need extra space to run around.

Lizzie looked up when a shadow crossed the blanket, and her mouth went dry when she recognized Brother Webster, their pastor. Wasn't it enough that God had made her painfully aware of her shortcomings? Was it necessary for Brother Webster to mention them, too?

The pastor smiled and dropped down onto the opposite end of the blanket. Lizzie tried to return the smile, but her lips felt brittle. Brother Webster's eyes crinkled. "How are you, Lizzie?" Compassion warmed his voice.

"All right, I guess," she mumbled, wondering frantically how much he knew about her disgrace. Without thinking, she blurted out, "Did my mother send you to talk with me?"

His eyes widened and he chuckled. "Actually, I was just making the rounds and greeting everyone here. I hadn't intended to single you out. It seems like you have something on your mind, though. Would you like to talk about it?"

Talking about how foolish she'd been was the last thing Lizzie wanted to do, but something in his tone softened her heart. Before she knew it, the words were out:

"Why doesn't God keep His promises to me?"

If she thought she'd shock Brother Webster with her question, she was wrong. His face was calm as he replied, "What makes you think He doesn't?"

Lizzie hesitated for a moment, then decided to plunge ahead. The question had burned in her heart for weeks, and if anyone could give her an answer, this man could. "The Bible says He'll direct our paths. Isn't that right?"

The minister nodded in agreement. "I can't argue with you there."

"It also says that He'll give us the desires of our hearts." When Brother Webster continued to nod, she drew a deep breath and ventured, "Then why doesn't He do that for me?"

Brother Webster regarded her thoughtfully, then said, "Instead of my answering that question for you, why don't we let God speak for Himself?"

He laughed gently when Lizzie frowned and looked around as if expecting some sort of divine announcement right then and there. "I don't understand," she confessed.

"You don't have a Bible with you, I suppose?" She shook her head, shamefaced.

Things went all wrong when she read the Bible and tried to put it into practice. She would leave that to people wiser than she.

Brother Webster didn't seem put off in the least. "Then let me give you a verse to look up when you get home. Can you remember the reference that long?" She nodded, hoping she wasn't overestimating her abilities. "It's Jeremiah 29:13," he told her. "Spend some time thinking about that, and if you still have a problem understanding, come back and we'll talk again, all right?" He pushed himself up off the blanket and continued circulating among the crowd.

"Jeremiah 29:13," Lizzie repeated to herself. The verse suddenly took on the importance of a lifeline, and Lizzie was determined to keep a firm hold on it.

Brother Webster hadn't sensed anything wrong with her, she remembered. It was her own guilt that made her assume her inadequacy was plainly visible. She lifted her eyes and scanned the crowd, wondering if that might hold true for the rest of the people there. Was it possible she'd be able to pick up her life and go on, in spite of making such a monumental fool of herself?

Occasionally she caught the gaze of one of the picnickers, who would smile in her direction. Lizzie would force a smile and nod back, feeling a tiny flutter of hope for the first time since Tom Mallory rode out of her life and her world came crashing down around her.

When the call came to line up to eat, Lizzie abandoned the pretense of holding down the blanket and made her way to the table. Shaking her head at several offers to let her slip into the line, she took her place diffidently at the end. Being here at all was a first step, she told herself. Getting in line was another. For now, she'd take things one step at a time and see if it was possible to regain some normalcy in her life.

Out of the corner of her eye, she could see her father rounding up the children. She supposed she ought to be helping him, but just now she wanted to savor the tiny bit of progress she had made. Her mother, helping to serve the food, beamed at her when she reached the table and handed her a plate. "Help yourself," she said gaily. "There's plenty for everyone."

Then, looking over Lizzie's head, she cried, "Why, Adam, how nice to see you! We didn't think you were going to make it."

Lizzie felt like someone had punched her in the stomach. She turned stiffly to find

Adam standing right behind her, plate in hand.

"I wasn't sure I'd make it, myself," he said to Abby. His brown eyes, though, focused on Lizzie, and that tingly feeling was raising goose bumps along her arms again. "But I hurried as fast as I could. I didn't want to miss this."

He looked behind him, where the line was backing up. "I guess we'd better move along," he said, smiling at Lizzie. "It looks like we're holding things up."

Lizzie came to herself with a start and moved quickly along the table, scooping various items onto her plate without regard for what she selected. Her cheeks were warm, and she hoped she hadn't made a spectacle of herself in front of all those people, just when she had begun to believe she might one day be able to hold her head up again.

Mercy, what was wrong with her? She had stood there, staring like a ninny at Adam McKenzie before everyone in the whole church. Maybe they hadn't noticed. Maybe they'd assumed she had been talking to her mother. Yes, surely that would be reasonable, she thought, breathing a sigh of relief.

But what was the effect Adam had on

her? He had been a part of the ranch ever since she was a young girl, and there had never been anything about him to set him apart from the rest of the ranch hands.

Adam had always been . . . just Adam, steady and dependable and always there but nothing more.

Lately, though, anytime he was near her, it seemed that every nerve in her body stood on end, and when he held her gaze with his, it was almost like a caress. Lizzie shook herself angrily, as though by doing so she could shake off that feeling. She ought to have learned by now that she couldn't be trusted to discern a man's feelings about her. She certainly couldn't decipher the look in Adam's gaze whenever it rested on her. Was it pity? Censure? She couldn't tell, and she wasn't sure she wanted to know. Either one would be impossible to bear.

Lizzie reached the blanket and cast a furtive glance behind her. Thank goodness! Adam had waited to speak to Charles and was helping him fill plates for the children. That was supposedly what she'd come along for, but at the moment, she needed some time to regroup.

She could be civil to Adam, she decided, but not overly friendly. There must be nothing in her demeanor to lead him to think she was throwing herself at him. After her disastrous experience with Tom, she wouldn't leave herself open to charges of improper behavior again.

Lizzie watched Abby leave the table and approach their spot with Charles, Adam, and the children, each adult carrying two plates and trying to herd their rambunctious charges toward the place Lizzie had chosen. Apparently Adam had been invited to eat with them. It was all right, Lizzie reassured herself. She'd had time to pull herself together, and she would handle the situation with grace and dignity. Beginning today, Adam and everyone else would see a new Lizzie Bradley, one who could be trusted to behave as a proper young lady.

When the children descended, giggling and squealing, on their picnic spot, Lizzie settled them firmly on the blanket near her and had them more or less subdued by the time the adults arrived. Charles and Abby sat opposite her, stifling sighs of relief, and Adam took his place next to Charles.

"How did we ever manage to keep up with Lizzie and Willie at this age?" Abby asked, shaking her head and laughing.

"I think the fact that we were a few years

younger may have had something to do with it," Charles answered with a twinkle in his eye.

"Charles Bradley!" The sparkle in Abby's eyes belied her ominous tone. "Are you implying I'm getting old?"

Charles gave an exaggerated sigh and looked ruefully at Adam. "You see what it's like being married? A man has to watch every word he utters."

"I'll try to remember," Adam responded with mock solemnity. His gaze rested once more on Lizzie, seeking the response he was sure he had sensed at the table only moments before.

Instead of the welcome he expected, she met his gaze serenely and included him in the conversation, although he could just as well have been one of the children, for all the attention she gave him. *Just like one of the family again,* he thought in disgust. The anticipation he felt all week at spending the afternoon in Lizzie's company faded away like a morning glory blossom at high noon. *If I had any sense, I'd have stayed with the horses.* Was he ever going to be able to make any headway with this woman?

On the way home, Lizzie rejoiced in her

newfound dignity. *Finally,* she thought, *I can be the person I'm supposed to be.*

She jumped out of the wagon and gathered the food baskets before her parents set off to take the children home. All three had been worn out from their frolicking and had fallen asleep on the drive.

Leaving the baskets in the kitchen, Lizzie hurried to her room, where she opened her Bible and eagerly sought the verse Brother Webster had given her.

There it was, Jeremiah 29:13: "And ye shall seek me, and find me, when ye shall search for me with all your heart." Lizzie blinked and read it over again, slowly. The last four words burned into her soul as if placed there by a branding iron — *"with all your heart."*

Lizzie thought back over the assumptions she had made concerning Tom. Had she sincerely sought the Lord with all her heart? The answer came swiftly, unequivocally — no.

Truth and conviction swept over Lizzie in a consuming tide, and she dropped to her knees beside her bed, tears pooling along her lower lids and spilling over to stream down her cheeks. What had she done? She tried to assess her actions ruthlessly. In all honesty, she had looked for passages that conveniently spelled out the answers she wanted without paying much attention to what the Lord desired. As long as He seemed to agree with Lizzie, she had been content to assume that she had found His will.

With all your heart . . . The words pounded through her brain. Where had her heart been? With Tom Mallory and his easy, empty promises, she admitted, writhing in shame. Hadn't her parents raised her to believe that she mustn't be unequally yoked? That marriage should only be to another believer, a godly man? How had she dared to take God's Word, that sacred Book, and twist it to mean that Tom was the right man for her?

She flipped back to Psalm 37, searching for the verse that promised her the desires of her heart. Yes, that's what it said; but this time, she also read the words before it: "Delight thyself also in the Lord. . . ." Not a blanket promise of "I'll give you anything you want, Lizzie," but "Delight yourself in Me, and I'll fulfill your desires."

It made sense, she thought miserably. If she were walking with the Lord, her desires would be His. Then He could give her what she wanted most because it would be in accordance with His will. How far short of that necessary condition she had fallen!

Lizzie groaned under the weight of conviction, and the tears poured forth anew. "I'm sorry. So very, very sorry," she wept into her coverlet. "I want to listen to You. Please speak to me."

It occurred to Lizzie like a flash of lightning across a dark sky that in pointing these words out to her, God *had* spoken and very clearly. "Thank You," she whispered, and the tears came again, but this time in relief and gratitude.

Chapter 18

Whap. Whap. Whap. With a final blow, Adam drove the last nail into the porch railing and stepped back to view his handiwork. The railing now stood tight and firm, where before, it had sagged slightly. Sufficient for a bachelor getting on in years, perhaps, but not good enough to set up housekeeping with a view to raising a family there. Not good enough for his Lizzie.

The porch was one of his final projects, the major structural repairs having been finished earlier. He walked slowly around the house, surveying the tight clapboards, the newly painted shutters, and — his particular pride — the addition.

There he stopped, hands on his hips, a lump of joy and pride swelling in his throat. The original house had contained one small bedroom situated next to the kitchen, with two even smaller bedrooms upstairs. After judicious planning, Adam had torn out an outer wall and revamped the design. Now the enlarged kitchen boasted a roomy pantry where the original bedroom had been. And upstairs . . .

Adam had to see it once more for himself. He entered the front door — noting with approval that it hung true and no longer caught on the floor as it swung inward — and bounded up the stairs with boyish exuberance. The landing opened onto three spacious bedrooms. Adam entered the largest one and made his way to the window. Leaning against the sill, he took in the sweeping view of plains, hills, and distant mountains. It was as beautiful as any painting he'd seen back east during his boyhood, he thought, only this scene was alive, vibrant, and constantly changing. He knew he could be content to view its grandeur for the rest of his life.

Turning, he surveyed the rest of the room. It needed a woman's touch, he knew, but the basic work had been done and done well. In his mind's eye, he could picture lacy curtains framing the window and the scene beyond, a braided rug on the floor, maybe a rocking chair in one corner. Yes, he thought, it would make a fine home. A fine home to share.

He needed some time to put on the finishing touches — a coat of paint here and there — and once more he was thankful for Charles's and Jeff's generosity in allowing him time to work on the house. After all was in complete readiness, he planned to lay his vision of the future before Lizzie. Surely by then she'd be ready to hear of his love for her.

Time to head back, he reminded himself. *Better do something to earn your keep.* The prospect didn't bother him. It was a pleasant ride back to Double B headquarters, and he could fill the time with thoughts of Lizzie.

Lizzie glanced up at the ruffled curtains hanging limply at her bedroom window. Not so much as a breath of air disturbed them, though her window was wide open, inviting whatever breeze there might be to waft inside. She sighed and reluctantly closed the Bible on her lap. She had spent a wonderful time with the Lord, pouring out her heart to Him and digging deep into His Word, but now the room was growing unbearably stuffy, and she could feel the beginnings of a headache coming on.

Even though she had made halfhearted efforts over the years to learn the domestic skills expected of a young lady, Lizzie was an outdoor girl at heart. Today the house seemed more confining than ever, and she hurried outside where the wide vistas and smells of summer beckoned. Her temples throbbed slightly, and she decided the effort required to saddle Dancer was too much, so she set off languidly on foot.

Settling herself under an enormous cedar within sight of the house, she decided that today even the outdoors wasn't much less stuffy than her room. Heavy clouds massed overhead, but instead of delivering rain, they only loomed oppressively over the landscape. No breeze stirred, yet the still air took on an almost tangible quality of its own. Lizzie loved the summer rains that brought freshness and renewed life; this sense of tension, of violence waiting to break loose, was something else altogether.

She turned her mind deliberately to the time she'd spent in Bible study. Had all those wonderful promises really been there all the time? Why had she never seen them before? Trying to be honest with herself, she admitted that she'd never done much looking before now. Even though she had become a Christian as a child, she had coasted along all these years without giving much thought to growing spiritually.

A passage about new believers being babies in Christ sprang out at her during her reading. She had become a newborn babe in Christ the moment she asked Him to be her Savior. More than ten years later, she could still remember the feeling she'd had that night — like she'd been washed clean. And yes, it was very much like she'd been reborn.

But babies, precious as they are, are supposed to grow. She tried to imagine what it would be like ten years from now if baby Susannah still lay helpless, wrapped in her blankets. Why, if that happened, she reasoned, Jeff and Judith — all the family — would be grieved beyond measure. Susannah was supposed to grow, to learn, to become less dependent on her parents and able to take care of herself.

The comparison struck Lizzie like a physical blow, startling her into wide-eyed awareness. For all her years of being a child of God, she had stayed a spiritual infant, dependent on her parents and others for her feeding and nurture, never bothering to learn to grow on her own. In a spiritual sense, she was little older than Susannah, still waiting to be fed and diapered. She shifted uncomfortably at the thought. How much had she grieved her heavenly Father by this lack of growth? she wondered somberly.

Lizzie scanned the panorama before her, where the sense of anticipation hung heavy. Even the slender blades of grass stood motionless, waiting for the release the storm would bring. God's creation spread out before her, vast and unending, and she felt as though God Himself was focusing His attention on the tiny speck that was Lizzie Bradley. The Creator and creation alike seemed to be waiting with breathless expectation. Waiting for what? For Lizzie to make the choice to end the years of infancy and take her first feeble steps toward growth?

Instead of bowing her head, Lizzie prayed with her eyes open, the better to fix this scene and this moment in her mind forever. "Father," she said aloud, "I've never really understood before. I know I've been Your child for years, but I never once thought about going beyond that. And I never thought about it hurting You." She paused a moment to order her thoughts, then went on. "I've been riding along on my parents' relationship with You, depending on their knowledge of You and not thinking that I needed to develop my own." She sighed, knowing the hard part was to come, but beyond it lay forgiveness and release.

"I'm sorry for taking You for granted all this time. Please forgive me for letting You down. With Your help, I'll learn to grow like You want me to. Thank You." A sweet feeling of freedom washed over her, cleansing and restoring her soul more than any number of summer rains ever could.

Lizzie rose and stretched, grateful that now the building storm was only outside and no longer in her heart. With slow steps, she retraced her way toward the house, happily making plans. Just how did she go about growing? Babies needed milk before they graduated to solid food. What did that mean in a spiritual sense? She couldn't wait to talk to Brother Webster and find out. Lizzie felt that a whole new adventure lay before her. Growth wasn't always without its pains, she knew, but it would be worth it. For the present, she would concentrate her whole being on her spiritual quest.

Adam McKenzie's face sprang into her mind, and it surprised Lizzie so that she stopped dead in her tracks. She rubbed her eyes, as if she could scrub the image away. Why was she thinking of Adam, with his unruly hair and melting brown eyes? Was this a temptation being thrown at her to stop her spiritual journey before it started?

Maybe it was time to deal with thoughts of Adam once and for all, she decided. She had known Adam since childhood and had seen him only as a routine part of the fabric of her life. Like the background of a tapestry, she thought, where the muted colors formed a regular pattern necessary for contrast with the central part of the design but didn't stand out on their own.

So why had this section of the background suddenly taken on brilliance enough to keep popping into her mind, unbidden and at the most surprising times?

Adam had stepped out of the background more than once recently, she had to admit. His name came up repeatedly in family conversations of late, although Lizzie had to confess she'd been so absorbed in her own thoughts that she really didn't know all that had been said about him. Papa and Uncle Jeff spoke of him with increasing respect, though. She'd picked that up unconsciously, just from the tone of their voices.

And it wasn't just in conversation that Adam appeared. He had sprung out of nowhere to rescue Willie the day her brother had played his horrible trick on her. *Or did he rescue me that day . . . from myself?* she wondered wryly. Then he came to her rescue like the most gallant knight of old when he found her alone after Tom's desertion. Lizzie couldn't remember that episode clearly, only that she felt safe and protected when he cradled her in his arms.

And lately . . . Lizzie's stomach did a flip-flop at the thought of how she felt when Adam's gaze bored into hers at the picnic, in the barn, wherever they happened to meet. Even when other people were around, their glances only had to meet and hold for Lizzie to feel that only the two of them existed. It was a pleasant feeling, but unsettling. Did her presence affect Adam the same way? Was it possible that . . . ?

Lizzie shook herself, irritated. Hadn't she learned anything? Tom's sweet words had taken her breath away. The touch of his hands on her face made her toes curl. But feelings weren't enough, as she had learned to her sorrow. The honeyed words were hollow, and by Tom's own admission, his hands had caressed other faces besides hers. What she had taken as a great love had been nothing more than a pleasant pastime for him. If that was the way men were, she determined, she would never again trust mere feelings for guidance. And Adam, she reminded herself with regret, was a man — a man just like Tom.

Wasn't he?

She wouldn't — *couldn't* — make the same mistake again. It was better for herself, for Adam, for everyone concerned if she devoted herself to growing in Christ. She needed to put Adam out of her mind and focus on the Lord. Maybe someday she could examine her feelings for Adam with some spiritual maturity. Until then, she would avoid contact with him. It was only fair.

Lizzie halted on the porch steps. *Poor Dancer,* she thought, *cooped up in his stall.* Even if she didn't plan to go for a ride, the least she could do was bring him outdoors for a breath of fresh air, such as it was. Her mind made up, she turned and walked to the barn. The poor horse must be as hot and miserable as she was. She would brush him down, fuss over him, and let him know he was appreciated. With Dancer, at least, she didn't have to worry about his affection being a product of her imagination.

Adam rocked along in the saddle, so

much at home there that keeping rhythm with his horse's gait came without conscious effort. The horse knew the way back to headquarters as well as Adam did, leaving Adam free to daydream. As the completion of his renovation drew nearer, so did the time he would be able to tell Lizzie of the life he envisioned — and how he hoped she would share it with him.

Adam played out various scenarios in his mind, rejecting them one by one. Lizzie had gone through a lot with Tom Mallory. Adam wanted above all to make her understand that his own intentions were beyond reproach and that he would be honored to be given the responsibility of caring for her for the rest of his life. The moment would have to be perfect.

He would wait, he decided, until the final touches on the house were completed. He had previously entertained the notion that with most of the work already done, it might be finished enough to let Lizzie see the results of his labor. Now he discarded that idea. It would be better to wait until every detail had been attended to.

How would he approach Lizzie on this? If she would consent to it, he might invite her to go for a ride, then take her to his ranch and get her reaction to the place first. Then he would have a better idea of how to proceed.

If he weren't working so hard on the house, putting in so many hours there in addition to his work at the Double B, he might have time to court her properly and build the relationship gradually. As it was, though, he was so busy building the beginnings of a life for them that there was no time for that.

Adam liked to do things properly and in order. Life dealt its share of changes to the plans he made, but he still found security in starting a project with a definite goal in mind. The problem with the current situation was that he really had no idea of Lizzie's feelings toward him.

He had been in love with Lizzie Bradley for years, since she was just a girl, and voicing feelings like that about his boss's daughter then would probably have gotten him thrown off the ranch, if not worse. It hadn't kept him from loving her, though. Nor from following her with his gaze, memorizing every facial expression, every gesture. He could close his eyes in the dark of night and call up a picture of Lizzie without any conscious effort. After all, he'd practiced enough over the years.

Adam sensed that Lizzie was feeling the first stirrings of womanhood before she had been aware of it herself. To Adam, it seemed like God's providence that his accumulated savings enabled him to buy the Blair place at just that time. He had taken it on faith that God was opening his way, one step at a time. To have Charles's blessing and support in this venture was an additional encouragement.

Adam was completely certain of his own feelings, and God seemed to be making the way plain before him. The only unknown in the whole situation was Lizzie herself and how she would react. In the past few months, Adam had known the heights of joy, then plummeted to the depths of despair, as Lizzie's manner toward him alternately warmed and cooled. The advent of Tom Mallory appeared to set him back immeasurably — at one point, seemingly forever — but now he could see how even that could work for good. If only Lizzie could see it the same way!

Her attitude lately puzzled him. The day he came across her in the barn, it seemed to him a magnetic force was drawing them inexorably together. And at the church picnic, he knew beyond a doubt that when their eyes had met and held, she was drawn to him as much as he was to her. Surely he couldn't have imagined that! Immediately afterward, though, she chattered to her parents and the children, hardly sending a word or a glance in his direction. He had to know where he stood and soon. The uncertainty was killing him. That was why his approach, when he made it, had to be done just right, thought out perfectly.

His horse's gait quickened, and Adam glanced up to see the ranch house and outbuildings coming into view. His heart nearly stopped when he recognized the object of his daydreams walk to the house, then pause and turn toward the barn.

Something shifted in Adam's brain. Maybe he'd been *too* methodical, *too* cautious. Maybe Lizzie needed to see a more spontaneous side of him. Without pausing to think things through in his usual way, Adam suddenly threw caution and all his careful planning to the winds and galloped down to the barn.

Exhaustion from the work he'd already put in that day rolled away as he swung from the saddle and threw his horse's reins over the hitching rail. He took a moment to run his fingers through his hair and tuck his shirt in snugly, then took a deep breath and strode into the barn.

★ ★ ★

Lizzie was leading Dancer down the aisle when she saw Adam enter. Her eyes widened at the sight of him, and her breath caught in her throat. She willed her feet to move forward, though it felt as though she were forcing them through a molasses-filled swamp.

It was a good thing she had just had that talk with the Lord. Knowing the way she felt around Adam, coming upon him so soon after he had once more filled her thoughts, might have left her dangerously vulnerable. And she wouldn't allow that to happen. It wasn't good for her, and it was hardly fair to Adam.

Adam seemed as ill at ease as she did. Normally the model of self-assurance, today he stood shifting his weight from one foot to another like a nervous schoolboy. What was wrong with him? Well, it wouldn't matter once she got around him.

If she got around him, she amended. Either he didn't realize he was blocking her way or didn't care. Lizzie cleared her throat. "Good afternoon," she said civilly, if coolly.

"Lizzie." Adam cleared his own throat in echo, looking distinctly uncomfortable as he twisted his hat in his hands. "I need to talk to you."

Even a good ten feet from him, Lizzie felt her breath quicken as that now-familiar tingling ran up and down her arms again. She didn't want to be rude, but it would be pointless to prolong this encounter.

"Would you excuse me, Adam? I need to get by." Adam shifted all of six inches to his right, and Lizzie sighed impatiently. There was no way she was going to try to squeeze between him and the barn wall. Not the way he affected her.

"Lizzie, please listen," Adam pleaded. "I wanted to wait to tell you this. I'd planned it all differently, but seeing you now, I can't wait any longer."

Lizzie stared, openmouthed. Where in the world was this heading? Had Adam done something he needed to apologize for? Even as the thought crossed her mind, she rejected it. If that were the case, he'd come right out and admit it like the straightforward man he was. Something in his entreating gaze touched a responsive chord deep in her soul. Warning signals flashed wildly in Lizzie's head. If she didn't watch out, her resolve would melt into a puddle right there on the barn floor and her newborn determination to grow in the Lord along with it.

She'd better try to get past him, after all, whether he moved over any farther or not. She moved forward, edging Dancer close to Adam to increase the distance between them. Feeling a flush of relief when she was past, she led Dancer quickly toward the outside door. Surely Adam wouldn't continue this conversation outdoors.

She hadn't counted on Adam moving swiftly behind Dancer and coming up on her other side. She whirled when his hand closed on her shoulder. "Adam, what . . ." Her voice trailed off when she saw the anguish in his eyes. "Are you ill?" she asked with dawning concern.

Adam dropped his hand and smiled sheepishly. "I do feel a little shaky," he admitted. "I'm doing this badly, Lizzie, and I'm sorry. I meant this to be something special, and I'm making a mess of it." He breathed deeply and began again, his voice husky with feeling. "In case you don't know it, Lizzie Bradley, you are one very special woman. I've known that for years. . . ."

His voice went on, but Lizzie didn't hear any more. The voice in her ears was not Adam's but Tom's, saying nearly the same words. *"You're a wonderful girl, Lizzie."* The words echoed inside her.

If she needed a sign, this was it. She refused to go down that path again. With a raised hand, she stopped Adam in midsentence, not knowing or caring what he was trying to say.

"Adam, I made a decision just before you came. I need to learn more about myself and what I'm supposed to do. I don't think we should be having this conversation."

Adam started as if she had slapped him, and a red flush stained his cheek as if her hand had indeed made contact. His lips moved, but no words came forth. His gaze probed hers as though trying to read her thoughts.

"You're sure?" The words came out in a hoarse croak.

Lizzie nodded. She couldn't think about God — or anything else! — when Adam was nearby. Keeping her distance would surely be the best thing for both of them. Without another word, Adam turned on his heel and strode out of the barn. Through the doorway, Lizzie could see him mount his sweat-stained horse and gallop away. She wondered briefly where he was going in such a hurry. It wasn't like Adam to overwork an obviously tired animal.

Chapter 19

After a week of Bible study and prayer, Lizzie had to admit that she had wasted years of her Christian life by not getting better acquainted with her Lord. Time spent with Him had become a precious part of her day, and she was steadily gaining a better sense of her identity in Him.

She also had to admit that having Adam out of her life hadn't been the relief she thought it would be. An overheard conversation between her parents told her he was spending time at his own ranch, wherever that was. Lizzie remembered vague snippets of talk about his ranch but had not really registered the fact that Adam had another place he could call home now, a place that wasn't the Double B. While she no longer had to contend with the effect he had on her whenever he was nearby, it didn't prevent her thoughts from turning to him again and again. Even prayer didn't seem to drive his image away, and Lizzie came to a startling conclusion — she missed Adam, missed him deeply.

In frustration, she decided to get away from the familiar surroundings for a few hours. Maybe some time spent alone with the Lord would enable her to make sense of the whole confusing situation.

Today she turned Dancer toward the northwest, deliberately choosing an area she seldom visited. She wanted to see nothing today that would evoke an emotion-laden memory. The ground grew rough, and she guided Dancer carefully around a maze of sharp rocks. *Father, I need this same kind of guidance. Show me what I'm doing wrong, and help me to know which path to take.* A depression opened up in the ground before her, apparently the mouth of a ravine.

Lizzie studied the opening. She didn't remember hearing of this place before. It was too steep and rocky for Dancer to try, but she was curious to see what lay within its walls. Tying Dancer's reins loosely to a tree trunk, she patted his neck, saying, "You stay here in the shade. I probably won't be a minute."

Lizzie picked her way through the undergrowth, hanging on to the trunks of small trees to keep her balance as the floor of the ravine descended at a sharp angle. What a wild, lovely spot this was! Once inside, it seemed she was in her own private world. It would be a perfect place to come when, like today, she needed to get away.

Stopping to catch her breath, she scanned the ravine. Sheer rock walls rose on either side, and numerous trees and bushes dotted the interior. Up ahead, it appeared the ravine made a turn, and Lizzie moved on to see what lay beyond.

When she was about to round the corner, Lizzie heard a sound ahead of her and froze. Was it a voice? But who would come here? Who else even knew of this place? She pressed against the wall, eased her head around the bend, and stopped still in amazement.

Adam knelt beside a large rock, his elbows propped on its smooth surface. His back was to Lizzie, and she strained her eyes to see who he might be talking to. His voice continued, and she realized with a start that he was praying. Embarrassed by her sense of intrusion, she started to slip away, then stopped short when she heard her name. Calling herself the worst kind of eavesdropper, she leaned her back against the rock wall and inched her head closer to the corner.

". . . don't understand it," he was saying. "Have I read everything wrong, thinking I saw Your hand at work when it was my own selfish desires?"

Lizzie blinked. Could someone as stable as Adam possibly have the same kind of struggle she had experienced? She tried to keep from breathing, wanting to hear every word.

"You know how I feel about Lizzie," he went on. "For years she's been all I wanted, all I hoped for. As far as I could see, You were working things out in Your timing. I've even thought lately that she felt some of the same things for me. But now . . . I tried to pour out my heart to her and she sent me away. Why, Lord? *Why?*" The cry sounded as though it had been wrung from the depths of his soul.

Lizzie trembled from head to foot. Adam took a shuddering breath and continued. "You ask us to sacrifice sometimes, but I never dreamed I'd have to sacrifice my love for Lizzie." He went on in a stronger, more determined voice. "If that's what You're asking of me, though, I know that You know best. Father, I lay my love for her and my hopes for our future on the altar before You. Help me to bear the loss if I have to give her up forever."

Lizzie pressed her fist against her lips to stifle a sob. She started to ease away but stopped once more at the mention of her name. "Please look after Lizzie, Lord. Guard her and protect her, and do what's best in her life. I trust You with that because I know You love her even more than I do."

It was too much for Lizzie. She crept back from the corner and made her unsteady way to Dancer. She gave the horse his head, not trusting herself to guide him when she couldn't see for the tears that blurred her eyes.

Adam loved her! The thought blazed across her consciousness like a comet. "Adam loves me." She said it aloud, testing the sound of the words. It still didn't seem possible. When had this happened? And why hadn't she known of it until now? Lizzie reviewed the years since Adam had come to the Double B, seeking some clue.

He had always been around when she needed him, always helpful, always polite. But a man in love? He never once let her know of his feelings, never showed any undue familiarity. He'd never even made an attempt to kiss her. *Like Tom did,* her memory whispered.

Yes, it always came back to Tom, she

thought wearily. Everything she experienced with him was what she had always thought went along with falling in love — the special way she felt when he looked at her with his sparkling eyes, her willingness to alter her own goals in deference to his. If that wasn't love — and it obviously wasn't — what was? She had good examples in her parents, also in Jeff and Judith. Their relationships contained strong feelings, she knew, but also were firmly grounded in the commitment to put the other's welfare first.

Like Adam? her relentless inner voice goaded. Yes, like Adam. Lizzie took another look at the years she had known him, approaching it from a different viewpoint. Looking at it from this new perspective, she realized that Adam hadn't found it necessary to pursue her physically in order to show his love. He had shown her in a hundred other ways.

When had the change come? Was there a moment when simple courtesy became a lover's tenderness, or had it grown up gradually, rooted deep like an oak? However it happened, it was a fact she could no longer deny. The words Tom addressed to her had been intended to deceive. Adam had poured out his heart directly to God, and she had no doubt of his sincerity. The question now was how she felt about him.

Lizzie thought about the way she reacted when Adam was near, the way a lightning bolt seemed to shoot right through her. It was similar to how she had felt with Tom but different, too. This was not so much sheer excitement as the feeling they were being drawn together, two halves that needed one another to make a complete whole.

She remembered the Bible stories of her childhood about creation, when God said, "It is not good that the man should be alone." Did that imply it wasn't good for a woman to be alone, either? Did that explain the aching emptiness she felt when Adam was no longer around? Was it possible — even desirable — that she could serve God wholeheartedly and allow Adam a place in her life, too?

Lizzie wrestled with these questions all the way home and long after she had gone to bed but not to sleep.

Chapter 20

Two days later, Lizzie had found some answers but was struggling with a new set of questions. There was no question about Adam and the caliber of man he was; everything about him was upright and true. Just as she had looked for the responses she wanted from God, regardless of what He wanted from Lizzie, she had been looking for the wrong things as proof of love.

And she could no longer delude herself into believing that a life of service to God meant He wanted her to live it alone. One honest look at her parents' godly example was enough to convince her of that. Lizzie shook her head slowly. How blind could a person be?

Now that she saw things clearly, she was plagued by the fear that in her fumbling attempts to do the right thing and protect them both, she had pushed Adam away so far that she had ruined her chance for happiness.

Even the memory of Adam's prayer didn't soothe her. She had heard him put the situation in God's hands. Did that mean he wouldn't come around again until God somehow took an active role to work things out between them? Now that she understood her feelings for Adam, Lizzie didn't think she had the patience or the courage to wait and wonder indefinitely.

But what could she do? She might be in love, but she was still so unsure of herself that she couldn't take the initiative and make the first move. It looked like an unsolvable dilemma.

Lizzie glanced outside for the hundredth time that morning. The clouds were still there, gray and threatening, promising to let loose at any moment. Apparently the rains had decided to come early today, and there would be no chance for a ride until they had gone. And just when she needed to be outdoors, to be alone and think!

Feeling that if she didn't expend some energy she'd explode, Lizzie went out to the porch and paced from one end to the other until she thought she'd wear a groove in the wooden planks. A few light drops fell to the ground, the forerunners of more to follow. Lizzie wanted to scream in frustration. If ever she needed to work off some steam, it was now, and she seemed to be blocked at every turn.

Maybe there was something she could do in the barn. If nothing else, the presence of the horses and the soothing smells of straw, hay, and leather would provide a balm for her troubled spirit. She dashed off through the raindrops, which were already increasing in force and number by the time she reached the barn.

Adam muttered to himself as he watched the sky and wondered if he should turn back. He'd picked a fine time to decide to apologize to Charles for taking off without warning. But then, he couldn't say any of his actions lately had been especially wise.

Look at the way he'd raced up to Lizzie and babbled about his feelings without any preparation, catching her completely off guard. No wonder she sent him packing! He must have looked like a wild-eyed maniac, descending upon her like that.

But running off like that . . . He'd told himself at first he was doing it for Lizzie, taking his unwanted presence away from her. In all honesty, though, he had to confess it was the blow to his ego that had done it. Initially, at least. Staying away had been nothing short of cowardice. He was afraid to meet Lizzie again, and that's all there was to it. Strong, self-reliant Adam McKenzie was afraid to face willowy Lizzie Bradley. He had faced her rejection once; he didn't think he could take it if she rebuffed him again.

It was time he faced up to that fear. If he was going to consider himself any kind of man, he had to go back. He still had responsibilities there, even if he hadn't been acting like it lately. And, he admitted to himself, it would be good to sleep in a real bed again, even if it was just a bunkhouse cot.

The proud owner of his own refurbished home, Adam had been sleeping on a pile of hay in his barn ever since running home with his tail tucked between his legs. After all the work he'd done on the house with Lizzie in mind, he hadn't been able to bring himself to take up residence there without her. *What am I going to do if she never comes around to my way of thinking? I can just see myself, twenty years down the road, with a fine house on the best horse ranch in New Mexico, spreading my bedroll out on the hay every night!*

Tiny drops of rain beaded on his saddle, and a larger one splattered across the bridge of his nose. *I should have known better than to come out when it looked like this.* He checked his location; he was about halfway between the two ranches but slightly nearer the Double B. That decided his course. He urged his horse into a lope as the rain pelted down in earnest.

Lizzie glared sullenly at the sheets of rain pouring down from the heavens. Coming to the barn had seemed a good idea at first. She spent time fussing over Dancer and polished her tack until the leather gleamed. Seeing that the rain hadn't diminished, she straightened the rest of the tack, rearranged the tools, and organized the feed bags into neat rows. The activity had helped use up nervous energy, but the rain was still coming down in torrents and showed no sign of abating.

She supposed she might throw a saddle blanket over her head and dash for the house, but she knew she'd be soaked to the skin by the time she got there. It looked like she was stuck where she was until the downpour slackened; she might as well find something else to do. She glanced around the barn and sighed. She'd been altogether too efficient. There wasn't a thing that needed fixing, unless she scattered tools, tack, and feed around and started in all over again.

Wait. Her gaze traveled upward to the loft. She hadn't been up there in some time, but being out of the line of sight, things were usually left in disorder up there much longer than down below where they were noticed. Lizzie nodded, relieved. She would climb up and get started right away.

Halfway up the ladder, Lizzie remembered why she hadn't climbed up there for so long. Her long skirt wanted to catch under her toe every time she raised her foot to climb another rung. She grasped the irritating garment with one hand, wrenching it loose and nearly throwing herself off balance in the process. The ladder teetered slightly, and Lizzie closed her eyes, waiting for it to stop before she went on. The agile cowboys had no problem here, but then, they didn't have yards of fabric wrapped around their ankles, either. It wasn't fair, she thought angrily.

The ladder ceased its swaying, and Lizzie climbed another step.

Adam could barely see ten yards in front of him. The last time the rain had come lashing down this hard was . . . well, he didn't remember a time he'd ever seen it rain like this. And here he was, caught out in the open.

His horse slowed, and Adam could make out dark shapes looming behind the sheets of water. He breathed a sigh of relief. They'd made it to the barn! He could hardly wait to get inside. Even if it took awhile for the rain to let up and he was stuck in the barn, he'd be under shelter, and that was all that mattered at the moment.

"Oh, isn't this just grand!" Lizzie groused. Now nearly at the top of the ladder, she had maneuvered her skirt out of the way long enough to put her left foot on the next rung, but as soon as she lifted the right foot, she knew she was in trouble. Somehow the fabric had wrapped tight about her right leg, holding her foot halfway between one rung and the next.

Holding tight with both hands, she looked down and sighed with exasperation when she saw the problem. The hem of her skirt had caught on a nail and was now stretched so tightly by her right leg that it wouldn't pull loose. Furthermore, it had somehow managed to wind itself around her leg and held it immobile. *Now what?* She couldn't stay up there indefinitely. Already her legs were beginning to ache. She reached down tentatively with her right hand, but the ladder started swaying so violently that she stopped, afraid to move again.

Lizzie surveyed the barn floor, trying to pick the best place to land if she fell, which now seemed all too likely. Unable to free herself from the constraining cloth to move either up or down, she would hang there like a fly caught in a spider's web until she could hold on no longer. Then she would drop like a stone.

If only someone would come! Even as the thought raced through her mind, Lizzie realized how unlikely that was. Who in his right mind would be out in this deluge? Twelve feet didn't seem all that high when one stood on solid ground looking up. Looking down from that height, though, gave a totally different perspective. How high had Willie been when he fell out of that cottonwood tree and broke his arm? Only ten feet or so, wasn't it? And he'd had a thick bush below to break his fall.

Her left hand, the one with the better hold, slipped a fraction.

Over the ceaseless beat of the driving

rain, Lizzie heard a steady *splash, splash, splash* and recognized the sound of a horse's hooves plodding through mud. Bert, she knew, had been out before the storm had hit. For some reason he had apparently come back home instead of holing up somewhere for the duration. It was foolish on his part, but Lizzie blessed him for it. If only he got to her before she lost her hold completely. She needed to get his attention; he'd never think to look up here when he walked in.

Twisting as far as she dared, she focused her gaze on the open door and called out as loudly as she could. "Bert! Hurry! I'm caught on the ladder and I'm about to fall!" She caught sight of a shirtsleeve as she turned back around.

The maneuver proved too unsettling for the ladder, which shifted abruptly to the right, loosening Lizzie's hold still more. Splinters dug into her hand as she made a desperate effort to regain her grip, but she was too far off balance now.

With a piercing scream, she plunged off the ladder, hearing the sound of ripping fabric as the hem of her skirt tore loose from the nail. She saw the knotholes in the wall flash by as she dropped downward — straight into a pair of muscular arms.

Lizzie squeezed her eyes tight at the moment of impact, aware only that by some miracle she was alive and unharmed. Then she opened them to look up at her rescuer and stared right into the face of Adam McKenzie.

Chapter 21

The impact of Lizzie's landing drove Adam backward, slamming him against the wall. He stood unmoving, staring back at Lizzie in astonishment. Lizzie suddenly became aware that Adam still held her and moved to pull away. Adam loosened his hold a trifle but kept her within the circle of his arms. Unable to continue looking into his eyes, Lizzie stared straight ahead, where she could see the pulse pounding in the hollow of Adam's throat, keeping pace with her own wild heartbeat.

"Are you all right?" he asked in a voice hoarse with worry. "What happened?"

"I'm fine," Lizzie replied, feeling anything but. "My skirt — it got caught on a nail, and I couldn't move."

Adam nodded as though it made perfect sense, then frowned in puzzlement. "What were you doing up there, anyway?"

Trying to keep myself busy so I wouldn't go crazy thinking about you, Lizzie thought. Aloud, she responded with a question of her own. "How do you always manage to be around when I need to be rescued?"

She saw the corners of his full lips tilt up ever so slightly in the beginnings of a smile. "Just lucky, I guess." Her scalp felt prickly when Adam slowly raised one hand and tenderly brushed a wisp of hair back from her forehead. Lizzie's gaze flickered up to his eyes again, where she saw her own sense of wonder reflected in their depths.

Adam's hand moved to her shoulder, slid down her arm, and clasped her fingers in his own. The tingle she always felt when he was near now seemed like a living thing shooting back and forth between them. He moistened his lips. "Lizzie, I acted like an insensitive clod the other day. Can you forgive me?"

Lizzie nodded, never taking her eyes off him. His smile grew a fraction wider. "Would it be all right if I tried to start over?" he asked softly.

She nodded again. This time she was ready to listen to every word he had to say. His grip on her hand tightened, and he swallowed nervously.

"Lizzie, I have loved you for years. I've

never told you before this because I didn't have a thing to offer you. But now, God has blessed me with a place of my own, a place where I can do what I know best — raise and train the finest horses around. It'll take awhile to get it into full operation, but I know I can make a go of it, and Lord willing, in a few years, it'll be known throughout the territory.

"The only thing that's missing is you. I can't guarantee what the future will bring, but I can promise you this — I will love you, protect you, and do my best to see that you're happy and cared for as long as there is breath in my body."

Without loosening his grasp on Lizzie's hand, Adam knelt in front of her. "Lizzie, will you do me the honor of becoming my wife?"

Tears welled up in Lizzie's eyes, but for the first time in a long time, they were happy ones. Joy and peace rose up inside her, filling every part of her being. Only one thing remained to be settled before she could give Adam the response he wanted.

She raised a trembling hand and rested it lightly on Adam's shoulder. "Before I answer, I need to know something. Can you forgive *me* for the way I behaved over Tom?"

Adam's brow creased at the mention of the name, and Lizzie plunged ahead before she lost her nerve. "I let him kiss me, Adam. Nothing more, but I did do that. I'm not proud of it — in fact I'm horribly ashamed — but I can't agree to marry you without knowing that you know and that you forgive me."

Adam slowly stood and laid one hand along the contour of Lizzie's cheek. "That belongs to the past now," he said, "and we'll keep it there. It's not only forgiven, it's forgotten." He released her fingers and cupped her face with both hands, tracing her cheekbones with his thumbs and staring at her as though he'd discovered a priceless treasure.

Lizzie thought she'd known joy a few moments before, but it was nothing compared to what she felt when Adam lowered his head and touched his lips to hers, gathering her to himself in a warm embrace. When he raised his head, he looked at her with satisfaction and declared, "There. That marks the end of that chapter of our lives and the beginning of a new one."

Lizzie nodded her agreement, too happy to speak. Adam's lips parted in a wide grin. "I take it that means you accept my proposal?" he asked her teasingly.

"Yes. Oh, yes!" Lizzie cried, hugging him tight.

Adam responded by wrapping his arms around her and whirling exuberantly around the barn. He didn't stop until he was dizzy, and they dropped onto a bale of hay, laughing giddily. "Do you think your parents will object?" His tone became serious once more.

Lizzie smiled and entwined her fingers in his. "God brought us this far," she said simply. "He'll see us through the rest of the way."

Adam slid his arm around her shoulders. "In that case, why don't we sit right here and make some plans?" He nodded at the undiminished rain. "It doesn't look like we'll be going anywhere soon."

Chapter 22

Lizzie Bradley, soon to be Lizzie McKenzie, looked out her window upon a glorious fall day. The sky, a flawless expanse of crystal blue, formed the perfect backdrop for the golden hills. Behind her, she heard a steady thumping sound and turned to see Judith removing Rose from Lizzie's bed.

"That's enough bouncing," Judith scolded her daughter. "Go find your father and see if there's anything you can do to help."

"I did," Rose protested. "He told me to come help you."

Judith rolled her eyes. "Then check with Vera," she ordered. "If she doesn't have anything for you to do, just remember to stay indoors, stay out of trouble, and stay *clean*."

"Yes, ma'am." Rose left the room, mumbling.

Lizzie chuckled, glad for the distraction. "Children are a blessing," she reminded her aunt impishly. "The Bible says so."

"Thank you," Judith replied with a grin. "I'll remind you of that someday."

Lizzie laughed, blushed, then laughed again. The door swung open again to admit Abby. "Are you ready?" she asked.

Lizzie nodded happily, raising her arms so her mother and Judith could slip the exquisite white dress over her head. The two women had labored long hours over the gown, fashioning a creation that took Lizzie's breath away. More wonderful than the beauty of the dress, though, was the love that had gone into its making. Carefully easing herself into the bodice, Lizzie watched the soft folds of the skirt settle around her.

Abby stooped to arrange the full skirt while Judith began fastening the long row of buttons in the back. "I'll get it," Abby said when someone rapped at the door.

It was Sam, wanting to know what he should do. "Go see what Travis is doing, and keep him out of mischief," Judith told him, rocking Susannah's cradle with one foot while her hands maneuvered the tiny buttons. "Honestly," she said as the door closed behind Sam, "I thought I raised them better. Is everyone else in this family completely helpless?"

Once more came the sound of knocking. "What now?" Abby exclaimed in exasperation. This time Jeff stuck his head into the room. He pursed his lips in a silent whistle at the sight of Lizzie, encased in the flowing gown. "Honey, you look gorgeous," he said and in the same breath added, "Have any of you seen Willie? He took off after lunch and I haven't seen him since."

"Do you mean to tell me that boy's run off today of all days?" Abby cried, her patience clearly slipping.

Lizzie's stomach knotted in panic. Willie was supposed to be Adam's best man. Surely he wouldn't take a chance on ruining her wedding!

"I'm sure he'll be back soon," Judith said soothingly, fastening the last button and giving Lizzie's shoulder an affectionate squeeze. She cast a stern look at Jeff and mouthed, "Find him. *Now!*" Jeff scuttled off obediently.

Abby lifted a garland of fall wildflowers and fastened it onto Lizzie's head, then turned the mirror so Lizzie could see. "Oh!" was all she could say. She felt the sting of tears. "Thank you, Mama. Thank you, Aunt Judith. It's beautiful."

"*You're* beautiful," her mother said gently.

"I'll second that," Charles said. He peeked cautiously around the door, then entered the room. "Would you ladies mind giving me a few minutes alone with my daughter?" Judith gave Lizzie a warm hug and an encouraging smile. Abby checked the dress, the garland, and Lizzie one last time, then enfolded her daughter in a wordless embrace before leaving the room with Judith.

"What do you think?" Lizzie indicated her attire with a lighthearted gesture meant to mask the sudden nervousness fluttering inside her like a host of butter-flies.

Charles regarded her with immeasurable pride shining in his eyes. "I think Adam McKenzie is one blessed man." Taking her hands in his, he looked down at her tenderly. "I can't believe this day has come so quickly. You are sure, aren't you?"

Lizzie nodded decisively. "More sure than I've ever been about anything, Papa."

Charles smiled. "You're getting a fine man. I'm happy for both of you."

Lizzie hugged him tight, heedless of her lovely dress. "Thank you, Papa. I love you."

The door opened one more time and Willie entered, his hair slicked down and clothes in perfect order. Lizzie felt light-headed with relief. Willie hadn't let her down; how could she have doubted him?

"Ma says to tell you it's time," he said, and Lizzie's butterflies returned, wings whirling madly. Willie cocked one eyebrow upward, and a slow smile spread across his face. "Not bad, Sis. Not bad at all." He gave her a wink and was gone.

Lizzie drew a tremulous breath and picked up the bouquet of fall flowers. Charles leaned near, offering his arm. She nestled her hand in the crook of his elbow and closed her eyes for a moment. *Thank You, Lord, for what You've done in my life. Thank You for the husband You're giving me. Help us both to grow in You for the rest of our lives.* She opened her eyes, squared her shoulders, and looked up at her father with a smile. "I'm ready," she said.

Rose waited for them at the end of the corridor, where Charles leaned far enough around the corner to catch the pianist's attention. As the strains of music filled the air, Charles gave Lizzie an encouraging nod, and they stepped through the double doors of the living room. Rose preceded them, solemnly scattering flower petals on her way.

The living room had been transformed for the occasion. Candles cast a soft glow over banks of flowers covering every available surface, and rows of chairs had been set up to accommodate the many guests, who now rose from their seats at Lizzie's entrance. Vera stood next to the aisle, beaming and wiping her streaming eyes with a handkerchief. Bert, looking uncomfortably stiff in his best clothes, stood next to her, and beside him Hank leaned on a cane, grinning for all he was worth.

Lizzie looked toward the front of the room, and the guests and decorations faded away. Her gaze was fixed on Adam and Adam alone. He stood waiting, tall and trim in his frock coat, watching her approach. When she reached him, she barely noticed Charles's kiss on her cheek when he placed her hand in Adam's and sat down next to her mother.

Lizzie heard Brother Webster's voice through a joyous haze as she repeated the vows to love, honor, and obey. But she and Adam, hands joined as they made their pledge before God, seemed to exist in a world apart.

Brother Webster stopped talking, but Adam and Lizzie stood staring into each other's eyes. The pastor cleared his throat and tapped Adam on the shoulder. "I said, you may kiss the bride," he told him above the ripple of laughter from the guests.

Any embarrassment Lizzie might have felt was forgotten as Adam embraced her for the first time as his wife, and his kiss blotted out everything but him and the certainty of their love.

The reception passed in a happy blur, with Lizzie and Adam accepting the congratulations of their friends and neighbors. Hank brought up the end of the line, nudging Adam in the ribs and saying, "I guess those pretty gray eyes will just be looking at you from now on." Adam flushed a dark red but managed to grin back and say, "You're a pretty sharp old codger, all right." He bent toward Lizzie and whispered, "Isn't it about time for us to leave?" Lizzie, glowing with happiness, nodded her agreement and hurried off to change while Adam went to hitch the horses to the buggy Charles loaned them for the occasion.

When she emerged a short time later, Adam was waiting for her, fending off good-natured wisecracks from Jeff and the cowboys. "Better hurry," he told her with a laugh. "I can't take too much more of this!"

The children crowded around, demanding to say their good-byes. Then Jeff shook Adam's hand and kissed Lizzie on the cheek, and Judith hugged them both. "God does have good things in store for you," she said with a smile.

"I know," Lizzie replied, her eyes alight with joy. "And I'm willing to let Him show me what they are . . . all in *His* timing!"

The others moved back, allowing Lizzie's parents to be alone with their daughter and new son-in-law. "Thank you for everything, Mama," Lizzie whispered, giving her mother a fierce hug. "Not just for today but for always." Abby, close to tears, returned the hug and nodded without speaking.

Charles stood in front of Adam, hands on his hips and a stern expression on his face. "Take good care of her, son. You hear?" Adam nodded, eyeing him steadily, and Charles's face broke into a broad smile. "I know you will, Adam. Welcome to the family!"

Adam helped Lizzie to her seat in the buggy, and she turned for one more look at her family and her childhood home. The buggy rocked and settled again when Adam climbed to his place and took up the reins. "Are you ready to go to your own home, Mrs. McKenzie?" he asked.

Lizzie started to nod but stopped at the sight of Willie coming out of the house. Crossing the porch at a run, he made a flying leap down the steps and came loping toward them. "Wait up!" he cried, waving frantically.

"It's about time," Lizzie teased him. "I didn't think I was going to get to tell you good-bye."

"You're running late for everything today," Adam said. "You had me plenty worried, not showing up for the wedding until the last minute." He studied Willie, who had climbed onto the buggy step and was dutifully hugging Lizzie. "Where were you, anyway?"

Willie looked up with innocent blue eyes. "Why, I figured with all the hullabaloo today, you might not have had a chance to tend to your stock," he said virtuously. "So I rode over to your place to make sure everything was taken care of." Lizzie shifted on the seat and eyed Willie uneasily.

Adam assumed a deadpan expression. "And was everything 'taken care of' to your satisfaction?"

Willie jumped down off the buggy. "It is now." He grinned and gave them a jaunty wave. "Have a happy homecoming."

Adam clucked to the horses and they moved away. "What all do you suppose he has lying in wait for us?" he asked with a rueful smile.

"With Willie, there's no telling," Lizzie responded. She looked up at her new husband and tried unsuccessfully to stifle a giggle. "I guess this makes you a full-fledged member of the family."

With the buggy cover shielding them from the view of the wedding guests, Adam gave her a kiss that told her how glad he was that it was true.

About the Author

Carol Cox makes her home in northern Arizona. She and her pastor husband minister in two churches, so boredom is never a problem. Family activities with her husband, college-age son, and young daughter also keep her busy, but she still manages to find time to write. She considers writing a joy and a calling. Since her first book was published in 1998, she has seven novels and nine novellas to her credit, with more currently in progress. Fiction has always been her first love. Fascinated by the history of the Southwest, she has traveled extensively throughout the region and uses it as the setting for many of her stories. Carol loves to hear from her readers! You can send E-mail to her at: carolcoxbooks@yahoo.com.